☛SOFTLY AS I KILL YOU☚

by

CHARLES NUETZEL

WRITING AS "JOHN DAVIDSON"

The Borgo Press
An Imprint of Wildside Press

MMVII

SECOND EDITION

☛Contents☚

☛Introduction☚

I have known Dan Benton for many years. He's a hard working private investigator, private eye, trouble-shooter, you name it.

The following book is his.

To give you some background about this man and how this book happened to come into being, I'll put down these few words of introduction.

He's cool-headed. Normally.

His line of work often involves following husbands or wives to see if they are cheating on one another. Usually he is lucky enough not to get involved in murder cases, though there have been some along the way.

When he came out of the service and attempted to get a job, it was to discover that he just didn't dig working under the thumb of others, following the book rules that big and little business require people to live by.

As a result, he decided to use what little knowledge he had picked up in his work in the armed service, via self-protection, via hand to hand combat.

Being a troubleshooter, his way of putting it, seemed like a logical means to make a living without being forced to work for others in a direct manner.

Bosses, he doesn't like.

Yet, when it comes to friends, he would lay his life on the line, give his last shirt or dime away. Because of this, his involvement in the following case was a highly personal one, starting as a result of his friendship with a long-time buddy who had saved his life.

As for women, they go for him, although he is not the

kind of man who openly comes right out and says it that way. He's a good looker. The kind of male females go for in a big way.

Yet, as he has pointed out, men in his line of work seldom, if ever, have beautiful young things throwing themselves at his feet every day, as suggested in so many detective novels.

It might sound hard-boiled at times, but his attitude toward life and women is highly refined and it is that of a total gentleman.

Even in telling me his story he was reluctant to reveal any more details than are outlined in this book.

It is enough to say that very few people are as loyal or as generous as Dan.

Being a writer, myself, I suggested that his experiences told here would make a very exciting book. Thus, we sat before a tape recorder and he started talking. I questioned him at times. Some of the conversations had nothing to do with the case. Cigarettes, booze and friendship cause side conversations to develop in a very natural way. So some editing and even restructuring were necessary to smooth out minor spots.

After having all of the story on tape the only thing required of myself was to get a secretary to transcribe the whole thing. After that, I edited and polished where necessary. When I showed the finished product to Dan, he had only one comment to make: "You're kidding? I didn't think I could tell it that way!"

That's Dan for you.

—CHARLES NUETZEL
Thousand Oaks, California
July 2006

❧Chapter One❧

Sherry Thomas is a great broad to have around any-time. Compact breasts that just beg for a man's caress. A body that wants more than just to be gently held; eyes eager, yet with innocence—plus several other qualities that make her worth having around. As secretaries go, she gives more than her money's worth. She's all for a little overtime—free of charge. Business or social.

When this whole thing started, we were in Las Vegas having a vacation in one of the high-priced hotels. Almost my last vacation, I might add.

Actually, we were in the dining room, beginning on a couple of cocktails, when my answering service finally got through to me. But my mind was still reviewing the last couple of hours we'd shared in the hotel room.

A man couldn't want more in a woman than Sherry. When she takes off her clothes, it can be like watching a high-class strip show. When she moves across the room, she has all the seductive qualities of a beautiful goddess in heat. With her it is all romance, a heavenly experience of giving— a gift of love.

As I sat at the cocktail table with her, my eyes focused on her revealing neckline, my mind was mentally caressing her, as my whole being had been doing earlier that day.

I was just reviewing the delightful ecstasy of her when I received the message from a scantily clad cocktail waitress that there was a phone call for me.

"You Mr. Dan Benton?" she asked, gliding up to our small table.

I couldn't help noticing her swelling, curving, lush

7

body that was packaged in a tight "bunny" type affair.

Yet Sherry would make her look like a formless kid, even in a sack dress.

I just nodded, hardly looking up.

"There's a call for you from Los Angeles," she announced in one of those low, breezy voices that women in her profession use too often in hopes of getting a large tip. A little innocent flirt here and a little flirt there and their pockets get as loaded as the customers at the gaming tables.

"You can get it at the desk." She was off before I could question her.

Looking back at Sherry and eyeing her reddish-blonde hair, then letting my eyes flow down the filled-out curve of her green dress, I took a deep breath and shrugged my shoulders.

"They seem to want to chase us all over the place!"

I had a pretty good idea what would be on the other end of the phone, and it would mean bang to our little weekend.

Two minutes later I was in a private phone booth, talking to my answering service.

"What is it, baby?" I demanded, setting my nerves against what was sure to be coming.

"Can you get back right away, sir?"

That was the answering service for you!

Right to the point.

It had to be important since I'd told them not to bug me unless it was a matter of life and death. But I knew the woman who ran it and we had been more than just speaking friends; the arrangement on the answering service was that they were like an extension of my own personal office—a back-up for Sherry.

"What's it this time?"

"Important. Or I wouldn't have bothered you, knowing how much you've been needing that vacation."

"Who's been murdered?" I asked dryly.

"More than that. Can't talk over the phone about it. But believe me, it's more than just important. Ralph Pentron needs you!"

"I'll catch the next plane in, honey," I announced,

and hung up before anything else could be said.

Ralph was one of the few human beings alive for whom I'd willingly lay my life on the line.

A moment later I had reservations for the next flight from Vegas to Los Angeles. There were about two hours to kill and it gave me just enough time to have some of the fun that had been planned before the phone call had interrupted what was supposed to have been a very long weekend.

I walked into the cocktail lounge and sat next to Sherry.

"Have to return to L.A." I let it lay there for a moment, watching the disappointment spread across her beautiful features.

"But we have a couple of hours before flight time," I added, and was rewarded by her warm smile. "Want to make time while we still have some?"

"Just time?" she teased. "Well, I suppose that could be considered my middle name—well for right now, anyway."

"Okay, Time, let's go up and make the hell outta ya!"

She nodded, and after I'd paid the waitress, we headed up to our room.

We'd come to Vegas to have a fun-time, now it was cut short. But sometimes quality comes in small packages, at least Time-wise. And her kind of Time was deluxe passion without any restraints. A very special woman.

And I sure, as hell, thanked the fella upstairs for having sent her my way, cause Sherry was the kind of broad that is able to take a man's mind off of all things other than her gift of love. And it was power-packed with a lush, stunning body that knows exactly how to totally capture a man in just about every and any imaginable way. Once we were in the room, she was all over me until I was all over her, and then we were all over each other, locked in a series of delicious embraces that enveloped our whole beings. Two hours can dissolve very quickly with that kind of action. It seemed only a few moments, and at the same time an eternity of beautiful ecstasy.

☛Chapter Two☚

The flight back to Los Angeles was one long, dragging experience. But the main thing was that we finally got there. I dropped Sherry off at the office with the promise that I'd have dinner with her that evening.

Even then, I had doubts about being able to keep the date. What possible complications could result in my meeting with Ralph?

The freeway traffic, as usual, was sadistically against human travel; it seemed as if every mile was hung-up with traffic jams. The temptation to take another route became so strong that I had to grit my teeth about one cigarette after another.

Thoughts shot through my mind like whip-lash strokes, replaying the years of friendship that were now driving me at a nervous deadline speed to a destination that was hopefully going to result in some defined conclusions. But I had no way of knowing what that might offer.

There are some people one knows in life who are so close that you will do anything to repay their friendship. Ralph was one of those guys.

We'd known each other intimately enough in the past to almost be of one mind. Plus the war experiences.

Sometimes that happens. Two people meet, be they of the same sex or not, and they have a mental contact that sparks a depth of loyalty.

It is enough to say that I drove with only a small portion of my mind on the traffic—the rest of my mind was puzzling over this urgency. What the damned hell had happened to cause Ralph to need my help so quickly?

Then twenty minutes later I was at the office of my

answering service, facing the tiny, compact Julie Martin.

She just handed me a note.

It had the following on it: "Call Ralph Pentron."

I raised my eyebrows questioningly.

"Get him on the phone," I directed her, turning and walking into her private office.

Two minutes later Ralph was on the phone.

"Ralph, Dan," was all I said.

"Can you come right over?" he asked in his high-pitched voice. The tone was solidly nervous, which was somewhat surprising. Ralph was always the level-headed guy who never got excited about anything. Even in battle conditions.

"Can you give me a little dope on the hit?" I asked. Meaning, tell me something.

"Not on the phone. How soon can you be over?"

I checked my watch. "In twenty minutes."

"Fine! Hurry! See you then." He hung up without another word.

All the way over to Ralph's my mind was reliving the moments in Korea, those last bitter battling days while the governments of the worlds tried to decide if they could bring an end to what seemed a useless war.

I was caught in crossfire from the enemy and then suddenly something hit me like a truck. I'd been struck in the chest.

Ralph was something like a thousand yards away, safe. I had heard, from others, how he had very calmly stood, ran straight towards me, got my body on his shoulders and dashed back to cover, receiving a bullet in the thigh and side, not stopping until we were in safe hands.

The two of us were side by side in the army hospital.

That, plus the normal buddy, off-duty times in bars and broads' bedrooms was enough to make any man feel a kind of personal liking for a guy. Beyond that, Ralph was hard *not* to like.

Such were my thoughts.

I arrived five minutes short of the time I'd told Ralph that I'd be at his apartment.

In the twelve years I'd known him I'd never seen

Ralph look so bad. He hadn't shaved. The clothes he had on looked like he had worn them for a week. His eyes were blurry and red-rimmed. There was the smell of liquor on his breath. His hair was all messed up.

"What's the bit?" I inquired, looking around the darkened room. The shades were down and there wasn't a light on in the place.

"Have a drink?"

"No—not right now."

"I need one," he announced, starting to walk over to the coffee table where there was a half-filled bottle of whiskey.

I abruptly stepped between him and the table, taking hold of his arm. "Simmer down!"

He looked at me like a desperate animal. "I need one, Dan!"

"Sit down and talk a bit." My voice was harsh and commanding.

He frowned at me, staring into my eyes for a long time. Finally he took a deep breath and then moved back. Slowly he went to a large leather chair and slumped down into it. His hands went up to his face and half covered it. He didn't say anything for a long time; just sat there, breathing heavily. Then finally his hands dropped to his lap and he looked up at me.

"It's a long story."

"I like long stories!" I moved to the sofa and sat down. "Blast away!"

Silence answered me for a short time and then he suddenly blurted out: "Somebody's trying to kill me!"

I jolted. Why in the world would anybody want to kill Ralph? The idea was beyond me. He just wasn't the type of guy to get into any kind of real jam bad enough to make anybody want to kill him. All his life Ralph had been blowing trumpet for a living, working with one band or another in town. He didn't need the money, because he was one of those lucky guys who had been born into a rich family. Music was just a living, lifetime hobby with him.

"Come on, aren't you being a little—"

"No! Believe me. I'm serious. Somebody's trying to

kill me. But it's more than that. It started some time back. I was working for Matty's group. Met this woman and then started going out with her. Betty Waters. We'd been seeing each other for a while; then her old boyfriend got out of the pen and that's when things started getting rough. The minute he found out about us, he flipped."

"So. What's the beef? I take it this Betty girl doesn't like him any more..."

"That's right but that's not it. This guy is a big timer. In the rackets and..."

There was a knock on the door, interrupting his sentence. He jerked upright. His face turned white.

"Don't answer it!" he whispered, shaking his head.

The knocking continued, and then the sound of a woman's voice came through the wood paneling.

"That's Betty!" Ralph exclaimed in relief, standing and moving to the door.

The moment he opened it, things happened fast!

Ralph was pushed forward and two men and a woman forced their way into the room.

The door closed.

Before I could do anything to stop things, Ralph got slapped across the face with a .38.

My knee-jerk reaction was stunned surprise. Then I moved into action.

Leaping forward, I swung at one of the men, but the blow didn't connect, much to my surprise. The guy ducked like a professional prizefighter. Something like steel hit my jaw and I saw nothing but a black whirling pit, throbbing and spinning into a painful ache.

I sank into a swift mental whirlpool with no escape. Like a dying man, reliving his life, having thoughts flash through his memory like instant replays, I watched a series of mental pictures flow rapidly into being.

Strangely, my own thoughts flitted from Sherry and our last moments in Las Vegas, to other women of the past.

I thought how it had been in her arms, how this loving woman was able to give so much and how much I wanted to give back.

I remembered my mother in her last years, when she

was old enough to have forgotten her interest in sexual men, yet young enough to want the male companionship that elderly people crave.

I remembered the generation gap all children feels is so important at one time or another in their lives and finally realize what a damned ass they've made of themselves.

I wondered about Julie Martin.

There was a woman for you. Yet I'd never learned just how much she might give a man.

I wondered about all the young girls I might have had romantic interludes with, but for some reason hadn't. Every man has those experiences. They grow up and learn that women, like men, require, crave love and affection. And sex.

I thought of the cruel things I'd been responsible for—innocent happenings done in thoughtless moments.

Then, most of all, I realized that I'd failed a great personal friend.

It was a strange experience that lasted perhaps less than mere seconds.

I was in a black, welling pit without form. Tormented mental visions were alive with pictures of all the people of importance I'd known.

My last thought was about how I'd failed to be the kind of person my father had wished me to be. He hadn't thought my kind of work was a very safe affair. Suddenly I couldn't help thinking that maybe he'd been quite right.

Then it was blacksville!

SOFTLY AS I KILL YOU, BY CHARLES NUETZEL

☛Chapter Three☚

Slowly the pit opened. I felt rough hands on me, but couldn't decide where they were touching my body. Then my eyes opened.

"Okay, he's awake," someone announced.

And then a very familiar face moved into my line of vision. Lieutenant Larson of the homicide division was glaring down at me. "Well, well, it looks like we finally have something solid to nail on your ass, Mr. Trouble Shooter, Dan Benton!"

From the pleased and crooked smile on the lieutenant's face I knew he was more than happy about the situation. Exactly what that was I didn't know yet, because my brain was still numb.

"What happened?" I mumbled groggily, starting to sit up. I tried to remember the last thing that had taken place before I'd received the "knockout" punch.

Then it came to me in a jolt.

"What the hell are you doing here?" I demanded.

"As if you didn't know."

"Sorry, buddy, but I don't!" I snarled, looking around the room. It took my eyes only a second to make contact with the very still body lying on the floor in the pool of splattered blood. Brains were exposed, raw and twisted, at the back of the skull where the bullet had made its exit.

Then a kind of shock set in.

I kept looking at the body on the floor and wondering what the hell was happening in the world.

All at once everything seemed senseless. Pointless.

Maybe in that instant I'd hit rock bottom.

I don't know.

But there was the body; *and it was dead!* Life had been stripped brutally away.

It was Ralph Pentron!

I felt sick inside. Nausea flooded over me and it was several moments before I managed to recover.

"Murder is always the business of the police department," Larson announced sarcastically.

"How'd you get here?" I demanded, trying to overcome my shock.

"A phone call told us about it. And damned lucky. It gave me the break I've been awaiting for a long time. A chance to nail something solidly on your goddamned slippery hide. Now I've got you exactly where I want you!"

My mind was still foggy or I would have figured out what the lieutenant was leading up to.

"I don't get you," I mumbled.

"Well now. What do you know about that, boys? The little man doesn't get us! We find him in the very act—no, excuse me, in a position which is almost as good—after the act—and he wants to know what it's all about!" Larson glared furiously at me.

"Oh, come on!" I cried, beginning to get the drift of the message. "Now how could I kill him? And then knock myself out...come on!"

"Just so that nobody can say I didn't give you fair warning, big shot," Larson continued as if I hadn't said anything, "I'll spell it out for you. I'm personally arresting you on suspicion of murder."

Under any circumstances that one can knock you out cold. It was something I just wasn't prepared for.

I looked at Larson, trying to believe he was serious.

The more I looked at him, the more convinced I became that he couldn't possibly be serious.

And the longer that feeling continued, the more sure I became that the truth was quite the opposite.

I started to say something, but the words didn't come out.

Everything was happening a little too fast for the human brain to adjust to even if you were some kind of human computer. And that's something I would have nothing against thinking myself as being.

I continued to look at the man as if I was mentally mindless.

His face grew even more serious. Maybe sadistic? I wasn't in any condition to tell the difference. Possibly he even looked delighted.

"Get me, big boy? Anything you might say can and *will* be used against you."

I considered making a break for it, then decided against such a foolish move.

It was all the law would need to be completely convinced that in some fantastic way Larson was right in arresting me.

There simply wasn't anything I could do but stand there fighting my own inner mental battle to believe this had happened.

And there was that other little item: Since *I* hadn't killed Ralph. I was damned sure that the guy who did would earn the price for murder. And I had some pretty good ideas where to look.

Continuing to stand there in a kind of dazed shock, I kept considering the two most basic facts facing me: Arrest and my need to track down Ralph's killer.

In that total state of mental confusion it was possible for a man, like Larson, to get away with any thing.

And he was.

But what would my own next move be?

If anything?

That, was the question.

And my hatred for the police officer named Lieutenant Larson grew to such burning fury with each passing moment that it took everything within me to keep from making hamburger out of his face right then and there.

And that's how the first few moments went after the announcement of my arrest for murder.

☛Chapter Four☚

I had always known that Larson didn't like me, but there is such a thing as taking a personal grudge a little too far. Sure, there had been several times when, from his point of view, I'd done things that "looked" a little underhanded. But when you have a client who's in trouble and you are trying to get him out, you do the best job you know how.

In the past there had been a couple of times when I'd had to pull some power ropes on a higher level than the lieutenant, and he'd been he fall guy. So what was I supposed to have done? Let my clients get shoved into some rotten cell for something they hadn't done? If the affair made Larson look foolish, that was his own fault, not mine! But there are some guys around who will never learn that they aren't perfect; some guys are never willing to take the blame for their own mistakes.

That was Lieutenant Larson. He'd been after my tail for years, and now he thought he'd bagged the king prize.

I looked blankly at him after he'd made his statement about taking me in for murder. It was unbelievable. Then I saw the determination in his eyes; a hard bitter expression. There just wasn't any room for doubt. He was deadly serious.

"You're kidding!" I couldn't help muttering.

"Not on your life! When the D.A. gets the evidence that you've been so kind to leave all over the place, you'll get the first degree murder joyride!"

"On what motive would I murder a good friend?" I said, standing up for the first time. "And what's more, how could I knock myself out?"

"Oh, we'll find one somewhere, don't you worry

21

about that!" Larson announced gruffly. Then he turned to one of his underlings. "Take this guy down to headquarters. I want him booked and then shoved into a cell! Got me?"

The man nodded and took hold of my arm.

I gave him a look and then said as evenly as I could manage, "Get your fingers off me!"

The guy's hand slowly opened and dropped to his side. "Just come along quietly, then."

"Who said I wouldn't?"

They cuffed me in a gruff, routine manner.

The trip to the jail was much too short. The booking and everything else that led me into a cell seemed to run too smoothly.

Finally my brain cleared enough to reason out that I had a right to make one call.

"I demand the right to make a call!" I told the man who had brought me to the station.

"In due time."

"Right now!" The words exploded in a harsh rasping sound.

He took his time deciding. "Right over there," he finally said, indicating a phone in the corner.

It was just a matter of seconds to get Sherry Thomas on the phone. "Look, baby, I'm down at the station—booked on murder. I know it sounds silly, but Lieutenant Larson has some queer idea about me. Pull a few strings! Get Davidson!" I didn't bother to tell her anything else; it wasn't necessary.

A few minutes later I was locked in a cell.

I had quite a bit of time to think things out—the call that I had gotten in Vegas; Ralph Pentron running around with a hood's girl; his being threatened with death.

Betty Waters.

What had she been doing setting Ralph up like she had?

That didn't make sense.

There had been a knock on the door. Then a voice calling. Ralph had said it was "Betty." No other "Betty" that I could think of.

Betty Waters had set him up. Under pressure? Why?

Questions.

Then the knockout punch! After that, the Lieutenant claiming that I'd murdered Ralph. But that didn't make sense either. Why would I murder a good buddy? How would I go about knocking myself out? And why blame me? Questions—without answers!

Larson had said something about a tip-off call to the police. Then, somebody must have set me up! That fact blurted out like a rocket spelling it out all over the sky. I'd been set up. Why?

Just because I happened to be there?

Another question: why had Ralph been threatened in the first place? Because of the girl? Or because of some other reason? And why—again—had she set him up for a death trap if she was supposed to be his girl?

It didn't make any sense at all. Just a few facts which didn't connect. So, where did that leave me? Behind the eight ball, in jail with a murder rap hanging over me.

A little string pulling would take care of the jail caper. There wouldn't be any difficulty getting me out on bail, at least. And then somebody better watch out! Dan Benton would be firing away and they'd better have one hell of a lot of answers for the questions!

But what questions? And who were "they?" Start number one: Betty Waters. Start number two: Ralph's apartment. Start number three: I'd seen the two men with Betty Waters, and if I saw them again I'd recognize them.

There wasn't much to go on, but that wouldn't stop me—only slow me down a little.

Somebody had killed a friend of mine. Then they had the damned nerve to tag the thing on me. And they are going to pay for it, and pay good and hard. Nobody does that to Dan Benton and gets away with it!

That made two counts that I owed the murderer—or murderers.

Even in my line of work, no matter how professional he might try being, one does get personally involved.

This was one case where, even without the obvious complications, I'd have been highly involved in an emotionally personal way.

23

But even then I needed to keep a cool head in order to reason out a puzzle that kept getting more involved by the hour.

Now, sitting there, brooding over my immediate situation, trapped, unable to make any useful moves to solve a problem that could drive the average guy into climbing the walls, I found myself desperately attempting to think of a way to get out of confinement.

I had never been the kind of guy that liked to be locked up. Any kind of set-up that restricted my movements became highly psychologically frustrating.

But there was nothing I could do but wait.

☛Chapter Five☚

Less than two hours after I'd been put into jail, I was called into Lieutenant Larson's private office.

He looked angrily up at me, his heavy face red and his eyes burning with fury.

"What's the meaning of this?" he demanded, slamming one heavy fist on the desktop.

I merely smiled back at him.

For a short moment I had the deep satisfaction of seeing the same angry torment in his eyes that I'd felt in my own mind. It is possible that this "torment" part was merely my personal need to feel he was somehow thrust in the same emotional bag I'd been in.

I glanced around the office, casually, trying to let on that his threatening posture wasn't turning me on, that I was calm as a happy newborn baby.

Cops can sometimes be highly irritating, even if they are routinely doing a good job. There are a few bad ones that make the whole force look sadistic and crooked.

It would have given me the greatest pleasure to thrust Larson right into the bag of a bad cop.

For some reason I couldn't help being tempted into thinking this just might be the case. Who knows? Some subconscious information or desire was pointing to this very possibility. The trouble with cops, good or bad, is you never know, for sure, if they were being tough simply in an honest attempt to do a good job or because they were rotten as hell. The job itself creates a lot of natural tension between those on the force and those beings out there called "the public"! Police work is difficult, and even the most dedicated cop can turn sour after a few years on the street. Some, of course, start out rotten and then improve their skill of hatred towards everybody who isn't part of the blue line. And there were even the downright crooked cops.

Somehow the idea of Larson being the latter had a psychologically pleasing effect on me. Certainly his attitude towards yours truly gave damned good indication that he wasn't necessarily on the up and up.

He banged the flat of his hand on the desk once more to get my attention.

"I don't get you, Benton. You can go pushing people around right in broad daylight and be set free as Christ himself, because you know some goddamned politician who pulls a few switches and pushes a few buttons. You can even get away with murder. But don't think that you aren't still in deep water. The only thing that's got you free is because we don't have any solid motive for you. As yet!"

He was half shouting in anger.

"You can be sure as hell and back that we'll have some kind of motive to slap on your hide. Then you're back in a cell—and the key thrown out the window! And I'll pull a few power lines of my own to see that you stay there—for good!" He was stabbing the air with his whole arm, half rising from his seat and glaring anger at me. Yet there was something about his words and anger and actions that seemed too showy. As if he was putting on an act for someone. Who?

"I'll get you—and that's personal!"

For a long time Larson just stood there, glaring at me and breathing heavily.

Then finally he said: "Get your ass out of here!"

"Sorry, buddy—better luck next time!" I threw over my shoulder as I moved through the door and out of his office.

I forced myself to forget it all, as I walked into the huge reception room where Sherry Thomas was waiting for me.

I moved to her and patted her shoulder affectionately. "Solid work, baby!"

"Tell me what happened," she asked.

"Over a martini."

26

She nodded, and we were off. Twenty minutes and two martinis later the story had been told. She re-invited me to her apartment for the evening, dinner included, and I said my "goodbye, 'til tonight". It was still early afternoon when I headed for the first phone booth I could find.

Looking up the name of Betty Waters proved a big mistake. There were more than half a dozen such names in the directory. That line of investigation came to a dead end, but quick!

The second possible line of action was Ralph Pentron's apartment. Without a second thought, I quickly headed in that direction, after checking my car out from "police care."

Sitting behind the wheel and starting the engine, I began working on the problem of getting into Ralph's apartment. Naturally I didn't have a key, and there didn't seem any easy way of talking the manager into letting me in the place. Of course I could try picking the lock, but there was the possibility of being caught and held for attempted burglary.

It boiled down to a matter of thinking up some kind of story. I could claim I was a relative. But the manager might have seen me earlier that day. Ad-lib it. That was the only thing that I could decide.

Finally I arrived; I parked the car and started up the steps nervously, wondering what to say, hoping I could think faster than the manager could.

The door opened, and a sweet-faced old lady looked out at me. Deftly, my mind ran across several possible lines of attack and then decided on the simplest.

"Is this the apartment of...where Ralph Pentron lived?"

She nodded grimly.

"Well, I'm a detective," which was only a partial lie, considering my P.I.'s license. "I just came from the department." Another twist of facts. Hell, okay, I'd been there earlier—jailed.

"They were here all morning..."

"I know that, but—there are a few other things. I'm a special investigator." I pulled out my wallet, opened it quickly and then closed it even faster.

She smiled and said: "Certainly. I'll get the key for you."

As she turned, I let out a deep breath of relief and then waited.

She returned a moment later and handed me a key. "The apartment closest to the staircase on the second floor."

"Thanks."

I started upstairs before she had a chance to begin wondering about my story.

A moment later I was walking into Ralph's room. I closed the door behind me and then started searching.

The desk first.

In the middle drawer was a little slip of white paper. On it were Betty Waters' name, address and phone numbers. All the information that I needed.

Twenty minutes later I was at the apartment house where Ralph's ex-girl friend lived.

The emotions charging through me were complex. She was probably not the type of woman to turn a man completely off.

I wasn't in any mood to try playing the "boyfriend" part—not even with Sherry, who was a natural favorite of this lover of women.

Ralph had always been the lover-boy and I knew damned well that Betty Waters was sure to be a hot comer. For any man!

And though I've never gone in for pushing a pretty babe around, I was completely in the mood to push somebody now, in order to get answers.

And that, my friend, was exactly what I expected— regardless of the price!

☛Chapter Six☚

Knocking on the door was the simple part of it. What followed was pure frustration. Trouble started with this woman who answered the door. And that was going to weave me into a completely complex web. She was beautiful. Almost breathtaking. It was the same Betty Waters I'd seen for that brief second in Ralph's apartment earlier that day. But this time I saw much more of her. She wore a blue robe. The large bulge of her brimming breasts held my attention for a moment.

Suddenly she recognized me. A startled cry broke from her perfectly shaped red lips that she instantly muffled with dainty long tapering fingers.

If I hadn't moved rapidly then, she would have closed the door on me. As luck would have it, my reflexes were faster than hers were and I pushed inside before she could close the door.

"You can't—" she cried in a desperately high voice, as I moved into her apartment and slammed the door behind me.

"Can't what, baby? I'm already here to ask a few important questions—and you better have the answers."

She backed away from me in terror, her eyes large and round and deep-blue. "But, you can't—" Her hand went instinctively toward her half-exposed breasts, trying to cover them.

"Oh, shut up and relax! I'm not going to rape you!" I snapped, pushing forward and reaching for her before she was able to get any further away.

For a long moment she stared up at me, her features working anxiously, her teeth biting her lower lip. "What are

29

you doing here?" she finally managed to blurt out.

"What'd you think? I'd be in jail for murder?" My voice sounded harsh and biting in my ears.

She just moved her head slowly up and down, and for a moment I couldn't help feeling sorry for her. Maybe I'm just a sucker for a beautiful broad, but there was something about her that made a man want to be protective—keep her from being harmed and hurt. Sucker males for a seductive, lovely lady.

At first my mind had been on what I had to say, more than what I had to see. Now I noticed the perfection of her body, and sudden desire forced its way up through my nervous system. Such is the automatic male response to visual stimuli. The "little guy" down stairs has no morality, it seems, it leaps up at attention!

My fingers relaxed on her arms and then my hands fell to my sides.

"Okay, just take it easy!" I said, half to her and half to myself.

By now she had noticed the direction of my gaze and a slight grin of satisfaction spread across her lips for the shortest of seconds. Then she frowned.

"I'm not here to hurt you," I said. "Just ask a few questions. You don't think that's too much to want, do you?"

She stood there, just looking blankly at me.

"After what your buddy-pal put me through...?" I added.

She didn't move for a long while and it was impossible not to realize that she was quite frightened of me.

"I said take it easy. I'm not going to harm you!"

"You have no right!" she started to say, then the words faded out. Stepping back and beginning again, she said: "You have no right to come in here and—"

"I'm already here, baby, so why don't you just simmer down and tell me something?"

She thought that over for a long moment and then relaxed. "I guess you do have an explanation coming!"

That was the understatement of the century. I had more than a mere explanation coming for what happened in Ralph's apartment that morning, and I was determined to get it out of her—by force if necessary.

"Blow away!"

"Where...where can I start?" she sighed, not looking at me now, but instead examining the floor in minute detail, as if she expected to find the answers there.

"Start with why Ralph was killed," I suggested in a slightly kinder tone of voice. By now my eyes were bouncing between her face and her rounded chest.

"Because of me and him," was her simple direct explanation.

"So why'd you turn on him?"

"I didn't!" she choked, looking up into my eyes.

"Oh, come on—out with it! I was there, remember?" Fury was building to replace the desire and heated lust that had been fanning the sexual energy inside me into a fiery burn. I could feel the tension build in my guts. I could see how my friend had found her such an attractive package. Any man would be interested. And my own body was churning at a high peak of natural, normal, automatic desire. Everything took on an unreal shade. Desperately I grabbed for her, my hands gripping the soft, giving flesh of her shoulders.

Without really knowing that I was hurting her, I shook Betty like a dog shakes a rag. "Out with it, you little—" I was about to say 'whore' but decided against it.

"You...you don't understand!" A sob caught in her throat for a moment and then her eyes misted.

I let go of her, suddenly aware of what I'd been doing.

It was a while before she could say anything else. But finally she looked up into my eyes. "You don't know what it's like being Jack Leiver's girl. You don't know...don't understand."

"Try me!"

"He threatened to kill me!"

"So you let him kill Ralph?"

Silence was the answer. Her lips were trembling and her face was white.

"Come on! Tell me more!"

"What? What else is there to tell?"

I thought that over. I knew the name of the man who'd killed Ralph, but for some reason something didn't click in the right order. It seemed as if something was missing and I couldn't put my finger on it.

Killed because he ran around with Betty Waters, the hood's woman. That didn't really figure. Ralph should have had enough sense to play it cool with the broad, not continue on into a death trap. Maybe he didn't really believe it.

But he'd been almost scared to death! It didn't figure. Didn't add up!

"What went on between you and Ralph?" I demanded suddenly. The effect was surprising.

She cringed as if slapped. "What do you mean?"

"What was with the two of you?"

"Nothing!"

"That's not the story that Ralph told me!"

"Well...we didn't... I mean we just went out a few times. That's all."

I knew she was lying, but there wasn't really any way of making her tell the truth without getting a little rough; and I didn't believe that this was so important, at least not at this point anyway. I hardly needed some pornographic detail of their sexual exploits. I wasn't expecting confession time.

"Look, baby, just don't blow the scene on me! Stick in town or I'll chase you down to hell itself if necessary. And see to it that you don't try getting away again! Got me?"

I turned and walked from the room. I'd gotten what I wanted from her. For the moment. All that I could get at this point. I was still shooting in the dark and there was a lot of ground that I would have to cover before I got all the answers that I wanted. But she didn't have all of them. Only the big man. Jack Leiver!

As I walked out to the car I couldn't help believing that things were a little too out of shape. It was all too easy. First getting into Ralph's apartment, finding Betty Water's address, and the information about Jack Leiver. Now it was simply a matter of getting to the little bastard who'd set this whole caper up.

That seemed simple enough—on the surface. But under that surface was something rough and boiling. That was what I had to find out. I had to be careful about it, too. It was the trap that could start clamping around me at any moment—if I made the wrong move. A trap that could spring without warning. That undercurrent. It was all too simple, and I didn't like the decayed smell of it all. It was just as if it were a trap set up for me to walk into.

My thoughts were anything but well organized.

I've been pushed around pretty much already.

By the police.

Now this Betty Waters was certainly playing the cool cat. I knew damned well she must be lying. Why? She had avoided answering that question.

I stood in front of my car for some time, torn.

Should I go back and get with the rough muscle on this bright little sexy doll?

She certainly wasn't the type a man wanted to push around. Usually he wanted to do something completely different to a babe like this.

And *that* kind of thing was completely out of the question.

Lighting a cigarette I continued standing there, attempting to figure out the next move.

With Larson breathing down my neck—no matter how subtly or bluntly, it wouldn't be smart to try pushing people around too hard.

But that was almost exactly what I'd promised to do when I went to see Betty Waters.

My trouble had always been being an all day sucker for a beautiful broad.

Sighing, I tossed the hardly-smoked cigarette on the cement and ground it violently out with the end of my shoe, getting a kind of sadistic satisfaction, which did little or no good.

At the rate I was going, a snail pinned down with rubber cement would beat me in a drag race.

SOFTLY AS I KILL YOU, BY CHARLES NUETZEL

☛Chapter Seven☚

Getting into the car and starting the engine, I determined to think things out a little more before pushing forward too far. I'd drive to my apartment, get armed and then try to reason matters out a little further.

First the phone call in Vegas. Ralph in trouble—because his girl was an ex-friend of a hood. That didn't make sense!

Why would anybody kill someone for such a weak motive? I couldn't help thinking that nothing was what it appeared to be

Then it suddenly hit me. Nobody would take a chance on a murder rap for such a small reason. Obviously there had to be something in this whole bit that hadn't come out yet. But why? Why had it been kept so damned secret? Or rather, why had Ralph not mentioned it right off?

Why would he just say that somebody was trying to kill him and claim that it was because he ran around with some sexy bitch in heat? And why had she set him up? She said that her life had been threatened, but that didn't add up, either.

Finally I arrived at my apartment and parked the car. Got out. Walked to my rooms and opened the door.

My mind was still in that mental daze of over-activity; almost blown-out by drastically attempting to find hard answers to impossible questions.

In such a state you move like a robot or zombie, blind to your immediate surroundings.

A dangerous mistake for a guy in my profession.

If you want some dumb advice from a cocky jerk, don't play the thinking game when involved in a problem

35

that requires total awareness of what is happening around you. I was in for a quick shock.

"Come on in, I've been waiting for you!" a voice greeted me from across the room.

My first reaction was to back out while the backing was still good. But then I saw the revolver in the man's hand and decided that this wouldn't, by any stretch of the imagination, be the best action to take. Instead I quickly moved in and closed the door behind me.

It was several seconds before I recognized the man standing there holding a gun on me. He was a dark fellow with deep-set eyes. One of the men who had come into Ralph's apartment!

"How'd you get in here?" I demanded, trying to make my voice sound a lot less concerned than it was—as if I was holding the gun on him.

He smiled and motioned with the weapon. "Sit down!" he ordered, ignoring my question. "I have a few things to tell you about the facts of life, and I want to have a good listener!"

I did as he demanded, taking out a cigarette and lighting it to give strength to my pose of self-assuredness.

"Okay," I stated calmly, "it's your play—make the most of it!"

"I intend to do that!" He kept the gun pointed at my chest, but his eyes circled the room. "Quite a layout you got here, buddy."

"It pays for itself."

"Speak when spoken to!"

This wasn't the time to argue. When a man has a loaded gun pointed in your direction it's better to play along with the gag. He not only had the gun, but I was sure he wasn't afraid to use it.

"Somehow," he started to say, directing his eyes back to mine, "you managed to get off the hook."

It took a few seconds for me to figure out what he meant, and then I nodded.

He smiled a thin mechanical expression of his lips. "You might be able to arrange things with the police, but I don't believe you are in quite the same position with the

36

Boss as you are with them." He let that ride for a moment and then continued. "I hear that you went to see Betty Waters. That was a very foolish thing to do, now, wasn't it?"

I didn't say anything to that; there just wasn't anything to say, since I felt it had been a very good idea. I'd managed to cause this second contact, without any personal effort. Here was one of Leiver's buddies. From the way he was now talking I knew he didn't plan on using the gun unless it was necessary, and that was one thing I didn't plan on making necessary! Smart-ass me!

After a few moments of silence he continued:

"What's your interest in this thing?"

"Why'd you frame me?"

"That was the boss idea. Leiver has some beauts. You just happened to be there, so he took advantage of it."

There was one of those silences again. They were heavy with nervous tension. For me, at least.

"What's the caper now?" I asked. That sounded almost convincing even to my own ears. Wanted to sound quite casual about this whole affair. No senses in letting the guy know just how shaken I actually was. "What're you all about, here and now?"

The man sneered. "For a guy in your profession you certainly don't use your head!"

"Scare job?"

"Bright boy!"

"I'm surprised that he didn't send more than one man."

"Didn't think it necessary." The man pointed to the gun with his other hand.

"Maybe you got a point there—and maybe not!" I was somehow managing to keep up the casual act, even though my guts were pounding like sledge hammers. "What're you guys afraid of?"

"The questioner, still?" The man moved forward and then stopped just about a foot away from where I sat.

Even if I'd been expecting it I wouldn't have had time to get away. Without any warning the man swung his arm and brought it across my face. It was a slashing blow that tore into the side of my cheek. If I'd had warning it would have been possible to soften the blow by rolling my head away from the swing, but I didn't have the necessary warning and got the full effect.

The world spun in a painful red. I felt myself shoot to one side of the chair and then an open hand whipped across the other side of my face.

It took several seconds to recover and then I felt a fist slam into the other side of my face again.

A dizzy spinning nausea overcame me then and I couldn't think straight for a long moment. Then the whirl-pool of blackness slowly cleared and I looked up at the man.

"That's just a warning, asshole!" he announced. "If you keep nosing around any more you'll find yourself really gone over by a couple of us boys. You'll feel like the biggest damn steam roller ran over you when they get through—so take this advice and keep out!"

With that he turned and walked from the room.

As the door closed I realized that his advice was plenty damned sane enough. A guy can't take too much of a serious battering and still live. The only thing wrong was that I was already in the whole bloody thing far too deeply to back out.

My mind was still too stunned to react properly. My body too numb from the sudden attack. But one conclusion did manage to race through me: nobody could do what he had just done to me and get away with it.

One thing was clear: there was really something hot blowing. Right under the surface. And once I'd cut through all that crap, maybe the reason for my friend's death would be blatantly obvious. The murder was one thing, all right, but there was one hell of a lot more. What, I didn't have any way of knowing—yet!

Weakly, I stood and moved to the bathroom. There was a little cleaning up to do on my face.

Then I remembered the dinner date with Sherry Thomas that evening. It had been a fool thing to arrange. It could be called off. But there was dinner, and maybe Sherry could put a little colorful lighting in the problem. Suddenly the idea of food and drink and a lovely loving lady to sooth my wounded body sounded very inviting, indeed.

I definitely was in this thing up to my neck, and there was only one way to get out—find Jack Leiver and find a way to prove that it was he who had done the killing.

And the motive?

That was a problem. I could almost see why Lieutenant Larson was so blown out of shape about not being able to hold me because of the motive problem. One thing that I could say about Larson was that he really was an honest cop—maybe too honest! For his own good, and for mine.

I cleaned up and by the time I'd had a couple of shots of whiskey it was just about time to head for Sherry's.

Well, we'd see just what happened. Maybe Sherry would be of some help in suggesting the next big step. She was a bright young woman who could do a little "detection" on her own. What I needed was a new brain on the problem—and she was elected. Of course that's part of why I'd hired her in the first place. Well, okay, the second place; the first reason had been the instant vision of her body as she walked into my office for the interview! That, alone, would have successfully landed her a job. Nobody would turn down such a lovely, intelligent and attractive package unless they were half out of their mind.

There's nothing like having somebody else to help you along when things get tough.

To say nothing about the added advantages Sherry could offer in an emotional way. Well, emotional is one way to putting it. A polite way.

I've always been a guy who finds female companionship highly rewarding in every sense of the word. There are all-too many guys who believe women are nothing but a sexual object to be used and thrown aside.

Me?

I'm different. I keep a winner like her around.

I can't honestly claim I'm some kind of authority on this or that I'm the only one in the world who has this kind of attitude about women. A lot of guys have gotten married for the same reason.

Me?

I'm not the marrying kind. At least, this wasn't my attitude concerning Sherry, though she is the first gal who would be in line—as far as I am concerned.

And anyway, of course, I'm not the type of guy who believes I'm God's gift to women.

Nonetheless, I looked forward to the softness of Sherry's lovely body, the gentle sweet understanding in her eyes, and most of all the emotional and mental ability she had to soothe a beat-up warrior after a long battle.

After all, that's the role real women have played throughout the ages. Take away the pain a sword-swallowing body has suffered. Oh, how lucky can a fella get?

Sherry's the perfect example of that!

☛Chapter Eight☚

It's funny what a guy will do under odd-ball circumstances. The last place in the world I should have been was at Sherry's apartment that evening. But it seemed, at the time at least, the only logical thing to do. Maybe people are directed in their movements by some destiny. I don't know; but this turned out to be a damned smart thing to do.

Sherry is one of those women who believes in being a woman. That is, she's not afraid to act like one. Knows how to cook better than most, and how to listen and how to talk.

When she opened the door and saw the condition of my bruised face she gave out a sigh of shocked surprise.

"What happened?" was her only question.

"Well, I can't tell you from out here," I announced, trying to grin and keep my eyes off the revealed sensually stimulating swells of her beautifully displayed breasts.

She noticed the direction of my gaze and smiled back. "I see whatever hit you didn't change that," she laughed, stepping back and motioning me in. "Feast away, if you must!"

I closed the door and then followed her down the hallway and into the front room.

There was a table set with a cocktail shaker and glasses.

"I need a drink—and bad. A lot of things happened since I saw you last."

"So I noticed," she observed, pouring martinis into the cocktail glasses. "One for you and one for me!" She handed one of the drinks to me and then saluted with her glass.

41

We downed half the cocktails and then I seated my-self on the sofa next to her. She didn't try to move closer or make any forward pass with her eyes or body. That's one thing about Sherry; she knew when to be physical and the right time to be mental.

This was only the 'mental-time'.

We sat quietly for a long while, and I started telling her all that had happened since I'd seen her that afternoon. When I'd finished, she nodded, waiting for me to start the questions.

"What I don't understand is exactly what—" I began.

"Why don't you call Davidson?"

"What the hell for?"

"He got you out of the jam today. Maybe he knows something about Leiver's activities. At least maybe he'd be able to get hold of the prison records."

That was Sherry for you—direct and to the point. Quick thinking. It almost made me feel like a fool. Maybe I was just too close to the problem.

"Seems as if Ralph wasn't telling you everything!" she added. Silence let that sink in.

"That's about what I figured. But what connection?"

"I should think this would be the first thing you'd have to work out—find out."

"I know. That's why I came up here tonight. After what's happened. Otherwise I might have been forced to call it all off. Considering my rather raw condition."

She smiled humorously. "You in the mood?"

I didn't say anything to that.

"You really hungry?"

"You bet. I need plenty of food and plenty of strength for the...well, let's say the investigation that's cut out for me from this afternoon's work."

"Don't fly off the handle, Dan. 'You know what—"

"Oh, come on. Don't be silly! I'm in this thing up to my neck and there's only one way out."

"Don't forget Davidson."

"Davidson might be a legal politician, but there are some things even he can't do for me."

"Like getting you out of a trial?" she asked, smiling.

"One thing to be pulling ropes and quite another to stop the unmoving machine called The Law!"

"Right, but he called this afternoon and said Lieutenant Larson has been yanked off the case because of the personal grudge he holds for you. He might have been anxious for a guilty verdict—too anxious. Item two: I hear he's still going to be looking around for any chance to get you on this deal—on his own time. Be careful. But the pressure is off."

"For the moment, you mean."

"For the moment, anyway. That gives you time."

"Big deal!" I groaned heavily.

Sherry stood and looked down at me. "They play rough!" she pointed out, examining my face.

"That's all you have to say?"

"What else do you want? Me to strip naked and let you make love to me?" she laughed, walking toward the kitchen.

"That's not such a bad idea."

"Be back in a moment," she called over her shoulder, disappearing into the kitchen.

As I sat there waiting for her to return, half listening to the sounds of her movements, I reviewed mentally the events of that afternoon.

The murder. The arrest. Talking to Betty Waters. Then finding the hood in my apartment when I returned.

Betty had called her boyfriend, telling about my visit to her place. She had called because she must have been afraid of what I might find out if I continued to run after her and Leiver.

What was it I wasn't supposed to find out?

Look over the facts.

Ralph had been seeing Betty while Jack Leiver was in the pen. He gets out, and trouble starts. Why?

Ralph had all the money he ever needed, so there wasn't any connection in that direction. Or was there? Had he been killed because he was seeing Betty? That didn't seem reasonable. But then nothing seemed reasonable about the whole thing. I was going around in circles.

I knew, now, that I'd have to return to Ralph's apartment and look the place over. There must be some clue there. What I might hope to find I couldn't even imagine. But it would be a start. There wasn't any reason for me to follow up the Leiver lead until I had more information. The chances of being caught by one of his boys and given a real working over for a reason I didn't know about wasn't appealing to me. If I had at least some idea of what was behind the thing, then it was worth the effort to find and question Leiver—with a little muscle, if necessary.

Reaching for the cocktail mixer I poured myself another drink and downed it, poured another and began sipping on it.

There was a lot more to this whole situation than I'd been exposed to, as yet. A lot of thinking to be done, too. And most of it had to be done in Ralph's apartment. I felt sure that that was where I'd find the real information that I needed.

And watch out for Lieutenant Larson, the hoods, Betty Waters, and one helluva lot of other things.

Leiver? Maybe the clue would be in the man's past. What had he been sent up for? And what racket was he in right then?

My head was spinning with questions and I wasn't getting any answers that could possibly fit.

The drinks were finally beginning to get at me, numbing the dizziness of my over-questioning mind.

Sherry walked in at this point with two plates loaded with food. And now my attention was turned in her direction. Maybe it was Sherry and her sexy walk.

My eyes went to her body and stayed there.

"Dinner's on!" she announced, sitting down in a chair at the small dinner table.

I thought—dinner? And that's for sure! I wanted to devour her.

Getting up and taking the tray holding the cocktail stuff, I moved to the table, sat down and filled the glasses. I handed her a cocktail and raised mine. "To you, baby!"

She smiled and downed her drink. I filled her glass again, gulped the rest of mine and refilled it.

The dinner conversation was dinner conversation. Had nothing to do with anything that was important. The only thing notable about the whole affair was that my eyes kept moving to the open dip of her dress, causing desire to swell upwards to a peak where I didn't really care much about anything else.

I wanted her. Just like that. Plans changed from running to Ralph's apartment first and then heading for Leiver's.

There is just so much the body can take—so much temptation.

The dinner finished, Sherry stood and started gathering up the plates.

"Leave it be!" I commanded suddenly. The drinks had finally hit both of us like a bomb. "Come here, baby."

Her eyebrows raised questioningly. "You kidding?"

"Come on over and find out!"

She came into my arms. Her whole body pressed almost savagely against mine.

Our lips met like fire. Moist and open. I felt her tongue reaching for mine so eagerly and anxiously that my reaction made me dizzy.

"Who said you were...sick?" she asked, pulling away breathlessly.

"Nobody!"

Without a word she took my hand, pulling me to her bedroom.

"Lover!" she sighed, starting to work on the zipper of her dress, "Help me?"

Now there's an invitation one healthy man is not going to turn down.

Especially one like me.

Making it with a woman like Sherry can be all love and kisses, romantic interludes of the highest order of class with a little wild erotic peak now and then to keep things completely interesting.

Now, being the kind of fellow who doesn't believe in going into details about his personal life; I think it's enough to say this much. That what Sherry was about to offer showed she really cared one hell of a lot about giving real help—exactly at the moment I needed it.

Enough to say she came through in flying colors.

Red, blue, green, white lightning and fiery oranges, yellows and you name it. Dynamite!

Later, when we shared cigarettes between us, a wonderful glow of pleasure flowed like caresses of a physical nature over each of us in the aftermath of our highly tender and loving expression of passionate and emotional giving. Okay. Raw sex! Wild and wonderful.

Little conversation followed that act. And that was of a personal nature, meant to fully rebuild the psychological wounds of this tired warrior.

If, through silence, she gave nothing more than that, it would have been enough.

I remember a fleeting moment when Sherry looked up into my eyes, tenderly reached out and caressed my shoulder, and said: "No matter what, Dan, come out of this in one piece. I need you."

That's the kind of thing any guy likes to hear. We had some more drinks, light personal conversation and once again discovered the warmth and beauty of one another's passionate love.

And with Sherry in your arms, brother, there's one hell of a lot of beauty to love.

From the first deep, throbbing kiss to the last sensual, lusting moment of ecstasy it was the perfection any man would wish from a woman he could truly love.

☛Chapter Nine☚

By the time I left Sherry's apartment the booze had managed to leave my brain. I was now ready for work. Getting back behind the wheel of my car, I found myself mentally returning to the problems that were sure to push me deeper and deeper into a pit of confusion.

I hoped to find some of the answers in Ralph's apartment. The problem of getting into his place was fairly simple. It was late at night, and if I was given enough time, and was quiet enough, I'd be able to pick the lock. If not...

I didn't want to think about that.

I'd left Sherry with a simple and basic assignment for the next morning: call Davidson and get as much information from him as possible. Information on Jack Leiver and anybody else who might pop into her mind that had anything to do with the events of the past day.

Finally I pulled the car to a stop in front of Ralph's apartment. Killed the engine and got out. A moment later I was in the hallway leading to Ralph's room Then I was facing the door. Reaching for the knob, to examine it, I was startled by one sudden, obvious fact—the door was unlocked!

My first reaction was that I'd forgotten to lock it when I left that afternoon. Breathing a sigh of relief, I pushed the door open and walked in.

That was the last thing that I remember for several hours. The room was dark when I stepped in, but the world became explosively darker. Something hit the back of my head.

Now I ask you, why is it necessary for people to go around using a guy's head for a baseball?

I don't think it is possible to go into the details of my forced 'sleep' again.

I know I kept thinking about how I should have stayed with Sherry and none of this would have happened.

Those thoughts, I guess, were a part of some kind of perverted sick dream of unconsciousness.

I hate boring the point too deeply, yet there is something about my nature which dislikes, in a violent way, being hit in the head at any time—let alone more than once.

Oh, why is it that man must make a living? Why can't we all have a paradise on Earth, without having to work so blasted hard to merely exist?

You tell me. I don't know.

The sins of the flesh. Maybe, just maybe, somebody up there was trying to teach me a lesson. If you stick your head out too many times it's just about going to be knocked off. If you don't, you just might as well stop trying to get ahead—because you ain't gonna get any rewards by simply sitting around on your fanny, collecting relief checks from the government.

Nonetheless, I'm really not all that much in favor of paying taxes for the pleasure of getting hit on the head.

Thusly ran the thoughts of a man in that unconscious state, where he is either on his way out or on his way back to reality.

At least, *this* guy's.

And as for tax money, I was beginning to feel as if somebody should be paying *me* a little bonus for the extra beatings that were hamburgering my body.

I was already beginning to hate having ever made a friend in my life who might get into trouble.

Realization of what was causing all this in the first place focused on my numbed brain.

And my determination returned like the force of an atomic blast.

Somebody was going to pay; and it would cost them. In blood!

I'm sure these thoughts ran wild in my mind on the slow fade-out and fade-in.

Like most humans I have a limited amount of

strength—and nervous energy.

Return to consciousness was painfully slow.

SOFTLY AS I KILL YOU, BY CHARLES NUETZEL

☙Chapter Ten☙

Then my thoughts really began to focus.

Being hit on the head one time in a day is one thing. To be slapped across your face at gun-point also the same day is something else again! To be slugged on the back of the head once more is just too much. To say that I felt a little pushed out of shape after being used as a punching bag not one time, not twice, but three times in the same day, would be an understatement.

The world had spun around my head for a long time. How long did I lay like that? There wasn't any real way of knowing. It seemed like a hellish nightmare through which I couldn't find any escape. Blackness throbbed and moved and wouldn't go away. I had conscious awareness for sometime before I was able to do anything about my body. My mind was working in a hazy sort of way for quite a while; that is, I felt like it was some kind of dream world where reality had disappeared. Then slowly things began to come into focus: I remembered having walked into Ralph's apartment and then having the lights of consciousness slammed out of me.

I jerked upright the moment that thought jolted through me.

My eyes were open.

I was staring into the semi-gloom surrounding me. At first I couldn't see much. Just darkness and blurry dark shapes.

I made out the furniture. The shapes were strange, and for a second, I couldn't remember why; then I remembered that I was in Ralph's apartment.

Painfully standing, I tenderly felt the back of my head. Whoever had done that to me had been in the room for no good reason. Had they removed anything that I might have come here to look for?

One quick sweep with my eyes around the room and I saw that the door of the apartment was now closed.

Walking to the windows I pulled the shades and then turned on the desk light. Nothing in the desk. Then the rest of the room. There was a table stand. Nothing there. There were several other places to search, but nothing!

By the time I'd run through the bedroom and the kitchen I was convinced. Whoever had hit me had really cleaned out the place. Lots of clothing thrown on the floors and things like that, but nothing that could tie Ralph with Jack Leiver and Betty Waters. A clean out!

And a bump on the head! Don't forget that, old buddy! The first time I discovered who was responsible for that little head work I was going to give it right back to them in full and then some!

Tiredly I moved from the apartment and then to the outside of the building; got into my car and drove it in the direction of my own place.

One thing was evident; I was giving somebody plenty of trouble, and they were getting scared. And that's what I wanted.

Because if they were scared, there was some reason to be scared; and that meant I was on the right track in thinking that there was more to this whole thing than seemed obvious.

Was Ralph scared to death because the girl he'd been seeing has a boyfriend who would kill him—just for seeing the girl? That might be possible, except for one thing; the girl had turned against him. If she didn't want to see Ralph it hadn't been necessary for her to play-act up to him like she had—or act as if she was still on his side.

Ralph had been killed maybe for some other reason! What? Why? Maybe I'd be getting some of the answers—or at least a few leads—from Sherry, after she'd talked to Davidson.

I arrived at my apartment, parked the car and went up to my room. Opening the door was one thing, the other was seeing what lay behind it. The place was in a shambles.

Completely upturned.

Fury slashed through me. What right did anybody have to do that? I cursed inwardly. What, in God's name, right did anyone have to walk into a guy's apartment and blast it out of shape?

Every drawer was opened and empty of its contents. Chairs overturned, furniture moved out of place. Books thrown all on the floor.

Whoever it was hadn't taken much time. They'd gone through the place as if chased by the holy devil itself.

One thought centered solidly into my brain: whoever it had been that had hit my head a little while ago in Ralph's apartment must have come here and done this.

But why? What had they been looking for?

Good questions!

Or had they been here first?

That was a thought that struck a strong cord of logic. They'd come here first, because they thought I knew more than I did.

No, that didn't figure.

That goon had been in the apartment earlier, after I was at Betty Waters' place. He had plenty of time to do this kind of work. Maybe he'd been sent back.

To hell with it! I thought angrily, starting to straighten up the mess, then I changed my mind. To hell with cleaning up.

I needed a drink and by God that's what I was going to have! After three straight shots of whiskey I'd had it. Sleep drifted down over my body, sending it into a soothing relaxed rest—a rest that I was going to be needing pretty damned bad. Because the trap had just started to squeeze around my throat. I'd just begun to feel the choking pressure of events.

If it ain't a girl to escape into the arms of, it has to be something else. Booze has its recovery effects, too.

Many times in the service, I'd boozed it out. Those years were a kind of yearly hell all their own. Men, like me, who can't stand the forced authority of being trapped in a kind of 'jail', will seek violent means to escape the mental and emotional torture.

When it wasn't some bar-fly, it was a bottle of booze.

Right then I needed hard liquor—not a woman anxious to make with the sack-game. I'd already tried that one out; and as rewarding as it had been, its ability to solve my problem of the immediate moment was nil.

Sometimes a guy simply has to cop-out, think things through in the frantic liquor daze that comes when you've blown several drinks too many into your brain cells.

Strangely enough, many answers magically come into being. Some useless; some powerfully effective.

I guess that's why the younger generation takes to pot and LSD. And drugs are their solution. They simply don't know any better.

As one guy socked it to me some years ago. He said, "When a man gets hung-up against the wall, he has only three ways to get unpeeled; a girl, booze or gambling." I'd tried two out of three.

Now it was boozeville, all the way!

☛Chapter Eleven☚

The next morning, after having breakfast out, I returned to my apartment and started cleaning up the mess that my visitor had made the evening before. I tried to keep my mind off the problem and the anger. There was one thing that I learned a long time before: if you try too hard to think things out, you simply don't get the answer. The subconscious mind just won't be pushed. The secret was to think about other things, giving your mind a rest, and then suddenly all sorts of weird things will happen.

There was something about this whole thing that I couldn't consciously put my finger on, but I knew that the subconscious must be aware of it because I was able to recognize something. What? I didn't know. If you can see something is wrong with your conscious mind, then you can be pretty sure that the subconscious has recognized at least a hint of what is wrong.

I had now reached a mental deadlock. The subconscious would eat away at what I already had and then when I'd gotten more information, it would mix it up with the answers it already had.

I'd just about finished cleaning when the phone rang. I was working so hard not to think, that the sound shocked my nervous system.

"Hello?" I fairly shouted into the receiver.

"Dan, Sherry!"

"What'd you find out?"

"Go on down to Davidson's as soon as you can. He wants to see you."

"What the hell?"

"Just said to send you on down."

55

"Nothing else?"

"Wouldn't give any information."

That shook me, but good. What kind of game was Bill Davidson playing now?

It didn't take long to finish the last touches on the apartment and then go down to the car. It was a short fifteen-minute drive to Davidson's office at the Civic Center in Los Angeles.

The minute I walked into his office I knew that more than just minor trouble was headed my way.

Davidson's face was grim and whitely drawn. He didn't smile or say anything at first. He just motioned silently with his hand for me to sit down. I sat. Then he let me have it. Both barrels!

In my condition I needed the gun-shot blast like a hole in the head.

Don't let me flop you out with details of a personal nature, but do let me explain that when a man like Bill Davidson decides it is time to make a move, you better watch out—and I wasn't in the mood for that kind of thing.

I stared at him, saw the expression in his eyes and knew that the next minutes were going to make life all the more wonderful for yours truly. *Like hell, it was!*

Just what I needed!

☛Chapter Twelve☚

Bill Davidson is a man of few words, except in court. As a lawyer, he wins a good many cases; he works hard and never plays around. If he says something, there is a very good reason for saying it. He means it.

He looked at me for a long while before speaking. His deep-set eyes kept to mine, and they seemed brooding and ill at ease. Finally he took a deep sigh and then asked: "What's your interest in this Jack Leiver?"

"Six guesses!" I snapped, feeling irritation at this unfriendly attitude that he was showing me. I'd known Bill for years; we'd been in the army together. Buddies, as the old book says.

"Can I give you a piece of advice?"

I nodded, half expecting what was coming.

"Don't. Don't do anything more."

"Oh, come on."

"I mean it, Dan." He pointed his finger at me to strengthen his words. "This is hot."

"So am I!" I shuffled in my chair.

"Take my advice and forget this whole thing. I can keep you off the hook...only if you keep out of this bit!"

For a moment I sat there in surprise. The threat—and that's what it was—stunned me. "Look, Bill. I'm giving it to you right off—straight. I got a battering yesterday. Three times. A good friend of mine is wiped off the map, and the blame is tagged onto me. I get knocked around for poking my nose into business that other people make mine and then everybody tries to get me to stop nosing around. What's the crap?"

"That's just it. Keep Out of the Leiver thing."

"I want him."

"You can't have him! And that's final!"

"Try to stop me!" I ordered, standing straight up.

"Sit!"

I remained standing, glaring down at Davidson.

"I told you to sit!" he commanded, stabbing the air with his finger, his eyes narrowing to thin slits. I'd never seen Bill so determined or angry.

But at what? I couldn't even guess. I sat.

"I'm going to let you in on a bit of information." He was silent for a little while, tapping the top of his desk with his fingers. Then his mouth started moving.

"You've made a bad mistake by stepping into something that's plenty hot. The F.B.I. has been working on this thing for some time now. If you step in any further you might mess the whole thing up."

"I don't get it."

"Leiver is in deep with the numbers rackets, just to name one thing. Also, narcotics. But we haven't been able to get anything on him. Except tax—that's what he was in for. He pulled a fast one and got out sooner than we expected."

Silence.

Then I asked: "What about Pentron?"

Davidson didn't say anything for a moment. Then his eyes met mine. "He worked for us."

That explained something.

"You mean that they..." I stopped in mid sentence. "Cut it, Bill. I won't go that route. That doesn't figure. Ralph was calling on me for help. He was scared that he was going to be killed."

The color drained from Davidson's face. Then he recovered. "Okay, if that's the way you want to play it, I'll just have to have the murder rap thrown on you again..."

"Come on, Bill. Let's not get dirty about this."

"You don't know what powers you're bucking!"

"Why the lie?"

"About what?"

"Ralph."

"Dan, he did work for us. That's the trouble. Why he came to you, I don't know. There's something about this whole thing that's got us all..."

"Why don't you let me work with you?"

"Can't. This is Federal work."

It took several seconds for me to let that sink in. "Bill, I don't know what I'm going to do or not do."

"Do me a favor and don't put your nose into this thing!" Bill Davidson looked deeply serious and concerned and worried. "I don't want to be forced into putting the squeeze play on you."

I didn't say anything else. I just walked out of the office. Burning anger shoved up through my guts. Anger at what Davidson had told me. Anger at what he had threatened to do if I didn't play along with him. Anger at what Leiver and his boys had tried to do to me, and had done to me. Anger at the whole goddamned mess.

Now the law had been pulled out from under me. Anything I did from now on would have to be all on my own. If I got into trouble it would stick. If I did do anything at all I'd have that murder charge slapped on me. Davidson knew that he couldn't make it stick, but it would stop me for a while. Long enough. I wouldn't be any good behind bars.

Maybe I should drop out.

I didn't know. All I could do was to think things out first, and then decide.

Think—that was all I'd been doing. Thinking and being batted around like a baseball.

Being basically a man of action, my thinking comes after the act. But in this thing the thinking was my only way. What next? The office? *The office!*

When I arrived I was in for one helluva big shock. Sherry looked up from her desk and then nodded toward my private office. "Somebody waiting for you in there." The expression on her face seemed slightly green.

"Who?"

"A woman."

"Who?"

"Betty Waters!"

I stared, trying to believe what I'd heard.

The look Sherry gave me then was either teasing or jealous. I wasn't sure.

"She's quite a looker," was her cool comment.

"So?"

She shrugged.

"What does she want?"

Another shrug met my answer.

"Oh, come on, Sherry, don't tell me you don't have any ideas?"

Her laugh was biting.

"And what does *that* mean?"

"What do you think my dear Mr. Dan Benton?"

"So formal?" I inquired, suddenly needing the fun of teasing her. How sadistic a guy can get?

"What do you expect?" She made a wicked face, then all-too lightly said:

"Of course, I could have suggested she stripped and made herself ready for my ever-loving playboy boss."

"Yes," I grinned.

"But I wouldn't do that, of course."

"Naturally."

"Don't you want to go in and have yourself a little fun and games?" she offered a little too freely.

"Are you inviting, offering or playing the lover's match game?"

"That's for television."

"Not for Sherry, though. Right?" I asked, moving around her desk in an attempt to let her realize the truth about my feeling for her.

"Don't you *dare,* Dan!" she exclaimed, in mocked horror.

"Then I better go on into the office and see what new virgin territory is in the offering."

"She's no virgin, I'll tell you that!" Suddenly I felt the impact of the serious point of the situation.

Frowning I said: "What was her attitude?"

"I think you better find out for yourself. This is your baby!"

"You're my baby, babe!"

"I meant, the *case,* " she pointed out quite seriously.

"I have a feeling there's something about to break and its waiting in your office to explode. Want any help?"

"I'll call if she tries to rape me."
"A promise?"
"Promise."
Then I turned and the lightness of games was over.
What the hell, was Betty Waters doing in my office?
What, exactly, did she have to offer now?

SOFTLY AS I KILL YOU, BY CHARLES NUETZEL

☙Chapter Thirteen❧

She was the last person in the world that I would have expected to want to see me. The hairs on the back of my neck seemed to prickle with excitement; or confusion; or maybe a little of both.

Giving Sherry a lecherous grin, I was rewarded with a flashing expression of jealousy clouding her pretty features.

"Don't you dare!" she demanded under her breath.

I laughed and moved into my office, keeping the smile on my face.

"Well, well, what have we here?" I asked, attempting to sound as flippant as possible.

Betty Waters looked at me in an odd way, her eyebrows moving together into a very attractive frown.

I could see what Ralph and Leiver saw in her. The way her body was almost held in by the flaming crimson-dress was something for the male hormone to really respond to. She had sex written all over her. The dip at the front of her dress didn't make any honest attempt to really hide the deliciously full, bulging curves of supple white creamy flesh. Then the way it hugged her shape and slid downward to a narrowed waist and flaring hips made my eyes fairly bulge in their sockets. She looked even sexier than I'd remembered.

I'm not a guy who normally reacts violently to a woman's body. At least, not in the way I felt myself fairly bursting with animal lusts as I stared at this woman standing in the middle of my office, looking at me with all the innocence of a small child.

Finally the frown faded and a full smile spread across her lips. Lovely and inviting. This was a new twist.

63

Quickly I closed the door behind me and walked across the office and to the back of my desk. "What can I do for you?" I asked in a very businesslike voice.

She turned and gazed down at me. For a moment she didn't say anything and then she leaned over my desk and smiled once more, this time making quite an effort to make it look sexy as all hell itself.

"I have a few things to tell you. Maybe you might be interested in hearing."

I raised an eyebrow.

"About Ralph Pentron!"

I nodded, trying to keep my eyes from finding her navel base, which was sure to reveal itself "nudely" to my rather anxious vision, if she dipped any lower.

"Blast away," I suggested, forcing my eyes down to my desk and nervously working my fingers on the paper-weight.

"Not here."

My eyes shot upwards. "Where?"

"Some place more private." She smiled and stood up-right. No more breasts peeking out at me.

"At my place?" she suggested.

I couldn't think of any place more private than my office, unless it was Betty Waters' private apartment. Even so I had the idea that I was either walking into a trap or into one hell of a party—a private party which would only have two people present; Betty Waters and myself.

The chance that it might turn into such a "party" made it well worth taking a gamble on my walking into a trap.

But what I wanted to know was why the sex angle? Why the play in the first place? Why her?

I couldn't figure it out. Why was she here? Why was she trying to make the scene with me? It didn't figure. But suddenly it didn't matter, either. I realized that I wasn't about to drop this case, regardless. Also I realized that if there were even a slight chance of "seducing" Betty Waters, I'd go all out to grab hold of it.

The why of the matter didn't count. A man had to learn in life to take what was offered and without questions.

64

If I started to question the motives of women, I'd never get to first base. Women want sex in any way they can get it, just as long as they think you believe they're "respectable." They like the sex play as much as men do. Especially if they are nympho. And I was beginning to think that Betty Waters was one of those women who would put out to any guy willing to take her.

That was beside the point. She had offered information. The requirement of getting it was going to her apartment. It could be a trap. It might be because the Big Boy had put her up to it in order to pump me.

That was a thought.

That would mean that they wanted to find out if I knew anything.

I looked carefully at her for a long time and then finally stood and slowly walked around the desk toward her. There was one sure way of finding one thing out about Betty.

I reached for her. Much to my surprise, she pulled away.

"I don't think that you want to do a thing like that, do you?" The expression on her face was one of pure innocence. But the smirk that was partly hidden in her eyes was something else.

"I don't know. Do you?"

"You never can tell," she finally smiled, taking hold of my hand and squeezing it gently.

This was silly, as hell. We'd only met twice, and under rather bad circumstances. The whole thing was wrong. I pulled my hand away from her and said, "Let's go on ahead. But business. I want to know what you have to say about Ralph, and that's the only reason I'm coming to your place!"

She just smiled harder, her eyes adding fiery taunt and tease to the expression.

I didn't know, for sure, exactly how I would react to her if she really made up her mind to make a play for me. I wouldn't be able to stop too many forward passes. But I'd decided one thing: that I'd been out of my mind to think of making with the double-whammies with her this afternoon. That just didn't make sense. And I couldn't understand what had caused me to even think about the possibilities. Maybe it was the sensual look and way about her. But there were just certain things that people didn't do—under any circumstances!

Forgetting Sherry.

Forgetting that I was a free man.

And forgetting that even under other circumstances there was something in the back of my mind that warned me that Betty Waters was something more than she was attempting to make me believe.

Nonetheless I couldn't help a slight teasing grin as I stepped into Sherry's outer office. Nothing like giving even your best girl a little something to worry about.

Like I said, people can be damned sadistic at times!

Can't they?

☛Chapter Fourteen☚

We walked from the office, past Sherry's desk and out the front door. All the way down the hall toward the elevator, I couldn't keep my eyes off Betty's swinging hips. They were moving wildly with every step. She had an almost animal look about her actions.

That might have been what had caused my mind to start thinking thoughts of wild seduction parties with Betty. She had every sign of a nympho, hot for bed.

The drive to her apartment was a long study in silence. Neither of us said anything; both of us smoked. That was all. Finally we arrived.

I was prepared for almost anything, from a trap to a bed party. The trap was out. And that left me slightly relieved; or maybe excitement was closer to the emotional reaction that I felt.

Once the door closed, Betty turned toward me. Her position so close to me, looking up into my eyes, left no doubt in my mind that if I reached out and grabbed her, she would willingly come up into my arms. But I didn't bite. Instead I moved away and stepped over to a large leather-covered sofa and sat down. Pulling out a cigarette, I lit it.

She stood looking at me for a long while, without saying anything. Then finally she walked across the room toward the kitchen. "Want a drink?"

For only an instant I thought about turning down the offer, and then changed my mind. "Sure. Anything you have."

She disappeared into the kitchen. I waited. Thinking. Why had she invited me to her place? And since that's what she wanted, why hadn't she just phoned me?

67

Two good questions and I was determined to find out the answers to both of them before I left her.

It only seemed a few moments before she returned with two strong-looking highballs. "Here you are, lover-boy!" she announced, handing me one of the tall glasses.

"Thanks loads!" I remarked, making it a point to keep my eyes off her body. I only looked into her eyes, but that was just as much a mistake, because there was out and out desire flaming in them. She smiled slightly, just a raising of the corners of her lovely lips. Then she sat down beside me—much too close.

"Bottoms up!" she saluted.

We tapped glasses and then I downed a good portion of my drink. Nervously.

For a long time neither of us said anything, but instead seemed wrapped in our own thoughts. Then finally a sigh uttered from her; it seemed to come from way down deep inside her chest.

I looked in her direction and found myself giving that whole body the third degree with my eyes. I couldn't help marveling over the hour-glass shape; almost like some artist's attempt to create the most perfectly sexual looking female form that he could possibly conceive. My eyes kept pausing at the large creamy cups of her breasts. My fingers sweated with their desire to touch those supple looking orbs.

"Okay, what'd you ask me over here for?" I demanded, turning away from her. I didn't dare look too long at that delightfully packaged bundle of sexual energy.

A light laugh bubbled out from her; it had a throaty, almost passionate sound to it. "What do you think?"

"Ralph!" I exploded in an argumentative voice; it seemed as if I was trying to convince myself, not her. It just wasn't right and proper to be here for any other purpose—no reason, no motive, no logic.

Except sex.

"Ralph. Oh, you wanted to know all about Ralph. That's right. I almost forgot." She was lying through her teeth.

"Cut it out!" I snapped. "That's not really why you got me over here. What's the real reason?"

68

"Whatever could you be talking about?" she demanded in a silky-high voice.

I turned to her and looked meaningfully into her eyes. "I'm no chump! You have some purpose other than the obvious. Not Ralph. That was the excuse. Not sex. That's supposed to look like the reason, but I don't buy it!"

She laughed at my face then. Her head moved back, exposing the velvet of her throbbing throat.

The temptation to pull her to me was overwhelming, but somehow I managed to keep control over my basically desperate needs to have it out with that body of hers right then and there.

"What's so funny?" I demanded nastily.

"Why you, Mister Lover-Man, Dan Benton!" she managed to gulp. "I've heard so much about the big hustler you were; all the wildest stories from Ralph. And all you are is a little guy with a big mouth and nothing to back it up!"

Something popped then in the back of my mind. Fury. Anger. Maybe it was only my subconscious mind seeking some excuse—any excuse—to make the hell out of her. My hands leaped out for her shoulders and yanked her close.

To my surprise she didn't resist, but rather melted into my arms, crushing herself against my chest. A sigh rushed from her parted lips.

The blood raced through every nerve and cell in me. I felt as if electric shocks had been charged through my whole body. Hot lava flooded my every muscle in that heated embrace. It was as if she were some evil witch from a far-gone age that had super-human power over males. Maybe it was the drinks. The build-up of many things. I don't know.

We parted, breathless.

She looked at me, a taunting grin spreading her lips. "You really are a man! I think we might just as well have some fun!" she suddenly announced.

It was utterly fantastic!

Suddenly, without really knowing how she managed it, she got my jacket off and then my shirt. Our passion worked up to such a pitch that we couldn't possibly desire anything short of ecstasy.

Then suddenly it was over as fast as it had begun.

The whole thing, as ridiculous as it all seemed. Why had Betty Waters come to my office? Why had she wanted me to come to her apartment? Why had she wanted me to seduce her?

I have ego, but not that much! Like any red-blooded human male, I'd like to think that it was just my winning charm and body. But that would be stretching things out just a little too far. After all, I've been around long enough to know the workings of life, at least a little bit. And this just didn't make sense from the very word go.

I sat up and looked down at Betty. She was lying on her back, her arms above her head, her eyes closed. The way her mouth was half-parted seemed as if she were posing.

I'd been brought there for some purpose. And I was beginning to get a bit curious about the matter. She'd bullied me into seducing her. I'd fallen for the simplest trap that women have ever sprung on the unsuspecting man.

Now I was determined to make things work out a little differently, even if I had to get rough. I meant to find out exactly what the real motives were behind this savage little sex bomb.

"Okay, cut the act!" I demanded in a brutal voice.

She went rigid, her eyes popping wide open. She frowned and then smiled slightly.

"Hi, honey," she cooed, reaching her arms up toward my head.

She shifted her position meaningfully, moistening her lips with her tongue. "So, you want a little more loving, lover-man?" she sighed, caressing the back of my neck with her fingertips. The contact was electric.

"Okay, baby, cut the bit!" I demanded in as steady and even a cold voice as I could manage under the circumstances.

She laughed knowingly and tugged on my neck.

"Cut the crap!" I ordered in a loud voice, slapping her arms from my neck.

A shocked expression clouded her features. "What the hell?"

"I want some answers!"

The smile moved back to her lips then, and she attempted, once more, to engage my neck.

Forcefully, I grabbed her wrists and slammed both arms to her side.

The expression on her face changed to surprise. "What's with you?"

"I want some answers!"

She didn't say anything, just looked up into my eyes.

"Why'd you bring me here?"

She moved slightly, trying to get free of me, but her efforts didn't do any good.

"Out with it!"

She laughed then. "What do you think? For your body!"

Without giving any warning I let one of my hands slap out across her face. I didn't like the idea of slapping a broad around, but this one was just asking for it. "Why'd you ask me up?"

I slapped the other cheek, and she moaned with delight. That surprised me. There was a fiery excitement burning in her eyes. A passionate wildness, verging on insanity.

A tremor ran across her body and she desperately attempted to press her hips against mine. In the struggle our bodies touched, then there wasn't any possible "questioning" after that. I couldn't have if I'd wanted to. Her body had complete control over mine. The mountain of lava flooded over me, holding me captive until it had finally passed.

I thought about Sherry and felt like hell.

But there are times when it is impossible to control certain more basic emotions.

Hellish, isn't it?

Poor Dan!

I felt like a bastard and knew that the next day I would hate myself even more.

And Betty Waters didn't help matters by saying: "You're the first man since Ralph that could turn little old me on."

That is just about all I needed.

Yet there is such a thing as ego in every man.

And sexual trips that a sex-kitten like Betty Waters was willing to take with a man, using that body like a tiger in heat, were in a word: "wildheat!"

I've always been a hard-working guy and never really found that the women in my cases were willing wantons in heat.

That's for the common detective novel. Pure fiction.

For a hard-working trouble-shooter like Dan Benton, having a woman like Sherry working as a secretary in the days and taking her womanly charms at night is just about all a guy can expect.

Unlike the fiction detective, where girls are always thrusting their stuff at them on every page, the real live-working private investigator usually has one hell of a dull time of it. Much of his work involves waiting in a car at night, watching and hoping something revealing will take place so he can go home and get some much needed rest.

But Betty Waters turned on full-force and before I knew it, we were involved in games not meant for kids to play.

And I was feeling guilty as hell, especially after having flashed that knowing, tease-grin at Sherry before leaving the office.

Maybe that's what made this case so interesting and frustrating.

Personally it was quite a startling experience.

And even more surprising was the way this woman that I hardly knew threw herself so anxiously into the intimate games only adults are supposed to play.

☛Chapter Fifteen☚

It was when I left Betty Waters' apartment that I really began to wonder what was going on in the whole "broad" world. There was one thing apparent to me: my world had gone crazy. People didn't act the way Betty and myself had acted. It was purely fantastic! I'd gone to her apartment for no good reason and gotten laid two god-damned times; stood from the floor and gotten dressed, and then without another word walked out.

As I drove toward my office I found it incredible to think about what had happened. Nothing had been solved by the hot interlude. I hadn't gotten any new information. I'd just been bedded twice by one of the hottest women in the world.

Why?

And none of my questions had been answered. After trying the one time, and then being literally seduced again, I'd given up.

But the point! What was it?

Nothing made sense. Nothing at all. Ralph's death. Being framed for his murder. Davidson giving me the squeeze play to keep my hands off the Leiver matter. Getting beaten up. Getting seduced. Getting pushed around.

It didn't make sense. And my mind needed some rest to think things out. Do a lot of thinking. And I didn't like the thinking gig. It was for the "eggheads," but there just wasn't anything else to do. I couldn't keep bludgeoning my way along without any rational action or reactions. I had honestly tried to question the broad and gotten nowhere.

It didn't fit; it didn't add up. And there didn't seem to be anything that I could do. I needed rest.

I looked at my watch. Office was closed. Sherry home. I decided to go on to my apartment for a good night's rest.

Twenty minutes later I arrived, parked the car, and went up to my place.

I was just tired. That was all. Exhausted. I stepped into my bedroom and fell on the bed. The world clouded to darkness and then almost at the same time I lost all conscious awareness.

I awoke with a start. At first, my senses weren't quite alive, but I was still aware of sudden danger; as if a sixth sense had awakened me. Shock jerked me upright.

The lights were on.

There were three shadowy forms standing around the bed. I couldn't, at first, make out their faces. Then I recognized the features of the man who had been in my apartment the other day—the one who had pushed me around at gunpoint. There was a crookedly triumphant smile on his hard face.

"What the hell?" I yelled, thunderstruck. Then anger rippled through me. "Get the hell out—you..."

Awareness jolted through me then. They weren't in my room for any patty-cake party.

"Just take it easy, my big-mouthed friend," the man said in a soothing silky voice. "We have a few matters to take care of." He nodded to the other two men, who without warning grabbed me, lifting me bodily from the bed.

One was on each side of me, and they had my arms pinned so tightly that the circulation was cut short. I was helpless in their grip. I struggled but it didn't do any good. They just waited until I relaxed.

"Okay, what's the goon squad for?" I demanded, beginning to get a pretty good idea of what was about to happen.

"Guess!" the speaker announced, stepping closer and leaning his ugly face a few inches away from mine.

Now I knew what it was like to feel like a trapped rat about to be put into the meat grinder of some scientist's experiment.

"Guess!" he ordered, his hand slapping across my

face. It was only a stinging blow; the beginning of what I knew was going to be one hell of a battering. But I'd gone through beat-meets before and lived, even if at the time I'd wished to high hell and back that I'd die.

"Guess!" he snapped, ramming his fist into the pit of my stomach.

I wanted to double over but couldn't. The two men at my sides were holding me tightly and upright. My guts tried to retch.

"You're about to wish you was dead!" the man growled, slamming the back of his fist savagely across my face. Then it jerked back across my other cheek.

The pain, for some reason, hadn't really taken complete effect yet. I was too mad. "You bastard!" I shouted.

"You're pushing the wrong guy when you try butting into my business," he growled, ramming his fist into my stomach once more.

My guts erupted up through my chest and out past my mouth. With very little effort I managed to force most of the mess to splatter in his direction.

He cursed insanely and swung. That was the last thing I was aware of for a long time, because he made the stupid mistake of giving out the final "Sunday punch." The stars exploded all around me and blackness took their place. Blackness and peace.

Throbbing awakened me.

Throbbing pain. My whole body ached. My whole body was in a vise of intense agony.

The lights blared in front of my eyes. I opened them.

At first I couldn't make out where I was. Time had stood frozen for me. I still thought fists were hammering me. Then I became aware of the fact that I was alone.

A moan trembled from my lips. I tried to move, but couldn't. Pain stabbed my body the moment I attempted to sit up.

A black hand clouded over my vision. Then grayness fluttered across all thought and all awareness.

How long I was unconscious I don't know. But finally I awakened again. This time I didn't return to the comfort of sleep. It was impossible to sleep now. The pain was too sharp. Too intense.

I attempted to move, but the only reward it got me was exhaustion and short aching breath.

For a long time I lay, silently thinking. Trying to make sense out of the whole blasted thing.

Why?

I couldn't come up with any answer that made sense. Everything that had happened to me the last two days didn't make any sense at all.

Ralph killed. The blame put on me. I get battered around. Davidson tells me to lay off the whole thing. Betty Waters shoots the sex at me, double time. Then Leiver hammers me to unconsciousness.

Why?

I was hitting a sore spot somewhere. Somewhere along the line everything tied together. But how? It couldn't tie together.

No! Start at the beginning.

Ralph is killed. The blame is placed on me. Larson is the man more than happy to arrest me. I get battered around when I do a little investigating on my own.

Did that tie in?

Ralph killed. Blame placed on me to get me out of the picture? When that doesn't work and I continue to snoop, they push me around!

But then, where did Betty's action fit? It might.

I felt suddenly sick inside. Everything was spinning and refusing to make sense. My body ached.

Slowly I tried to sit up.

With effort, I was able to.

I had one thought burned into my brain: I was going to blast this whole damned thing wide open if it killed me!

As things were going, it looked like it just might happen that way.

If you have ever seen a guy about to go insane you have a good picture of my mental and physical appearance.

Now I simply didn't care what it cost, who got pushed around or how many hamburgers I made out of men *or* women.

A guy can take just so much.

SOFTLY AS I KILL YOU, BY CHARLES NUETZEL

I'd just reached my limit.

SOFTLY AS I KILL YOU, BY CHARLES NUETZEL

❥Chapter Sixteen❥

I discovered that it took more than I had to get into good physical condition. In fact it took more than I had to even be able to move around. I managed, breathing painfully, to get to the phone and called Sherry's apartment.

Her sleepy voice answered: "Hello?"

"This is...Dan. Have a Doc...come over to my place. Hurry!" I told her in a weak, agonized voice. Then without another word I hung up. My head was throbbing like a thousand hammers were pounding it from all sides at once, and I was feeling the same pulsing ache all through my body. Sweat was dripping from every pore. I felt dizzy and my vision was as blurred as all hell. Finally I managed to move back to my bed and then slammed weakly down onto it.

A long time passed. I don't know how long. It seemed forever. I knew I was feverish. My mind was exhausted but wouldn't sleep because of the pain that stabbed every cell in my body.

They had done a good job—after I'd lost consciousness! For that I swore to get him, but good!

The trouble with books about private dicks is that they are fantastically unrealistic. A man takes a bloody battering, fighting it out with three or four thugs; all but gets his damned guts battered all over the place, until they resemble hamburger, and then he goes off to his girl's apartment and makes love throughout the long heated night. That's just not possible! After the body has taken a beating like that, a guy doesn't feel any more like sexing it up with some broad than he does to go flying to the moon and back without a rocket or space suit. And even if he wanted to—it wouldn't be possible.

I wanted to lie there and just die. Nothing more. After all the physical and emotional and mental effort and energy it had taken to get to the phone and back, I couldn't even think straight, or care about thinking.

Finally, the doctor arrived with Sherry. He took one look at me and dryly commented:

"What steam roller did you walk under?"

I managed half a smile, but didn't say anything. The first thing he did, after giving my body the old probing-finger routine, which was painful as all hell and back, was to give me a shot in the arm. A few moments after that I was drifting in sleep land like a baby. I don't remember much of the next day. I slept most of the time. Once or twice I awoke and was fed by Sherry. Nothing more.

Then, finally, one evening I awoke again and stayed awake. Sherry was in the other room; I could see her walking around.

"Hey, honey!" I called to her.

She stopped her movements and walked into the bedroom. "Oh, I see you're awake."

"What do you think?" I smiled.

She didn't smile back. Her whole attitude was all frosted business. "That's good."

"Is that the way to greet me?"

I was feeling swell now, and it didn't seem right that she should be the way she was acting. Not after what she'd obviously been doing for me.

"Well, you look good enough," she announced without humor. "So I guess you'll be okay from now on. I'll call the doctor. He said to get hold of him the moment you really came out of it."

I tried to sit up and discovered that I was still too weak to move.

"Just don't move around. You took a bad beating," she announced, in a somewhat kinder tone of voice.

Then Sherry walked from the room without another word, going to the telephone extension in the kitchen.

As I sat there looking at the place where she'd been standing I tried to understand the reason for her cool attitude. It didn't make sense. Sherry was an affectionate and warm woman—not cold and chilly. But, I reasoned, maybe she was just tired.

Anyway, there were other things to worry about that were more important than Sherry. More important than women and their strange impossible ways.

There was the beating.

Fury and anger rushed up through my whole body, flooding every nerve and cell.

Leiver was going to wish to hell and back that he hadn't taken the time and effort to knock me around. I'd get him where it was sure to do the most good, for what he'd done to me. With great pleasure I'd grab his balls and simply crush them to death.

What about Leiver?

That was the problem. The real one, in fact. Clear myself of the murder bit, by catching Leiver. Then I'd give him a little push-job all my own.

But why was he making such a deal out of this whole thing? I had to get out of bed and start shoving a few people myself. I was fed up to my ears and back with being a pro- fessional punching bag for every frustrated sadistic bastard that wanted a little excitement.

The doctor came, and in a few moments he gave me a fair bill of health. "You'll be fine in a day or so."

"I can't wait that long!" I argued back.

"You took quite a beating. Want to tell me—"

"No! I don't want to tell you about it. What's going to happen if I start running around—right now?"

He shrugged, looking down at me. "That's up to you. I can't keep you in bed by force...but you took a banging. At least stay in bed for the rest of this day!"

"Can't!" I announced, trying to get out of bed.

The world spun dizzily.

"Guess I'll have to," I sighed weakly, grimacing as I lay back on the bed.

"That's good!"

I must have fallen asleep right then because the next thing I knew I was alone. It was dark outside.

I lay in the bed for a long time, thinking. Trying to decide exactly what my next move was.

Betty Waters might be a possibility. The only thing was that damned sex bit.

The idea of sex suddenly didn't do anything for me I had the feeling that after what I'd been through, maybe I might be a little numb to her more basic appeals. This could be the best time to make the push job on her.

There was Leiver.

He was the guy I wanted. He was the guy pushing me around. He was the guy that I wanted to push back.

How long I lay there in the darkness, I don't know. But finally, I sat up. I was surprised to discover that my body didn't hurt as much as I thought it might. In fact I felt pretty good, considering.

Stepping from the bed I walked across the room and picked up a pack of cigarettes from the dresser. Lighting one, I tried to outline, in my mind, exactly what I planned to do. What I planned to attempt to find out.

Get Leiver. I could go direct, but I wouldn't have all the information that was necessary to make it worthwhile. I had to keep in mind that Davidson wanted me "out of the picture." If I moved, I'd better have a damned good reason. The logical thing was to see Betty Waters—if possible.

Everything was one gigantic question mark.

Everything circled back to Betty Waters.

Maybe that last was because she was such a whoring doll. A man is a man, and there isn't any getting around it that he is attracted to a beautiful broad.

Anyway, it didn't matter. Betty Waters had information that I didn't have, and I meant to have it before bungling any further into this mess.

I looked at my watch. It was three in the morning. No chance of getting anything done right then.

That's when I thought about Sherry.

Walking from the bedroom I started looking for her, expecting her to be in the apartment. To my surprise she wasn't there. That didn't figure. She'd helped me all these... I suddenly realized that I had no way of knowing if it had been hours or days. Anyway, she'd been here all that time, nursing me; and now she was gone.

Walking into the kitchen I went to the cupboard

where my liquor supplies were stored. There I pulled down a fifth of whiskey and poured myself a shot. Downing it in one gulp I was surprised to feel the powerful reaction which it had on my body. It no sooner hit my stomach than it had a rebounding numbing action in my skull.

The effect was startling. It all at once made me tired; so tired that I was forced to actually stagger back into bed.

I awoke with the sun shining brightly in my eyes. My whole body felt alive and vital. The minute I was awake I got out of bed, dressed and then left the apartment.

First stop: Betty Waters.

And this time I was determined that no bed games would be part of the action.

She'd taken me once, too often, for a sucker.

Now it was time to play the game my way—and for keeps.

After that, I'd hit the damned town for what it was worth. The answers had to lay some place.

Up until now, I'd been played for the sucker by all concerned and pinpointed as the number one bum target.

I was determined that, by the time I finished with Betty Waters this time, things would be completely different.

Such is the power of one's creative thinking under pressure. What happens in reality is all-too many times quite the opposite.

Of course.

Softly As I Kill You, by Charles Nuetzel

☛Chapter Seventeen☚

The drive to Betty's apartment was filled with mentally confusing questioning. And it got me nowhere.

I parked the car a few doors down from where she
lived, walked back, up to her room and knocked.

No answer.

I waited, thinking that maybe she was asleep. Then
knocked again.

The silent treatment.

Another series of knocking got me exactly where I'd
been before—with a silent answer.

Shrugging, I walked away, outside and back to my
car.

Now where to?

The Office?

Davidson?

The office!

Fifteen minutes later I was stepping into my office,
looking across at the cool expression on Sherry Thomas'
face.

"Hello, baby, aren't you glad to see your old lover?"

Her eyebrows lifted coldly. "I believe you've found
yourself another playmate!"

For a moment I couldn't understand what she was
talking about. Then remembered how I'd walked out of the
office the other day with Betty Waters.

Then I laughed. "What's with you, baby? That was
business!"

"Some business!"

"Oh, come off it! You know how it is!" I cried, half
angrily, stepping toward her.

"Oh, I know how it is!" she admitted in a superior voice. "You just aren't attached to any one female and just jump along from one to another. Like a rabbit! You don't fool me, Dan Benton!"

It was so foolish sounding that I couldn't really believe that she could be serious. After all, she didn't have any binding rights to me. We'd been in bed, but that's what we both had wanted. She was just another sexy broad that happened to also be my secretary and was willing to put out a little overtime, free of charge. What else did she want?

But then I saw the expression in her eyes and realized that she was quite serious.

Shrugging helplessly, I changed my personality to the pure businesslike attitude she was giving out to me. "Any calls? Or business?"

"No," she answered in a curt tone of voice.

"Okay then!"

I turned and walked out. Right then I was pretty damned irritated. Women! Give it to them in bed, and they think they can make demands on you! But I didn't go for that kind of female crap! I was free. And intended to remain so... Yet the very fact that I was mad made matters even worse. There were more important things to be concerned with.

Walking down to the saloon in the same building with my office, I sat on a bar stool and ordered a double shot of whiskey.

The minute the drink arrived I gulped it down fast, paid the bartender and walked out of the place.

Going to my car I drove to Betty Waters' place. Walked up to her room and knocked.

No answer; like before!

Where the hell, she could be at this hour of the day I couldn't imagine. Unless she worked for a living, which didn't seem very likely, considering the type of woman she was. With her looks, she could have a man keeping her.

Suddenly I realized that I was up a deep end. I could either sit and wait or go out and look up Leiver.

I decided on the latter. It was the best chance I had to start things moving. Maybe, I reasoned, I'd been wasting most of my time running around chasing my tail and getting no place. But the closest distance between two points is a straight line—not a circle. Betty was the circle, Leiver the straight line.

Starting the engine of my car I directed it toward the nearest telephone booth. Parked. Walked to the booth and started thumbing through pages of the telephone directory.

Leiver...Leiver...Bill, Walter.

No Leiver, Jack!

Next stop? Where?

I pondered that question and thought about Davidson, but quickly chopped that one out.

Betty Waters was my only link to Jack Leiver. And I had to find a way to get to her. Wait for her. That was the only thing left. Wait and hope she turned up soon.

I drove back to her apartment. Walked up to her room; knocked. No answer. It looked like it was going to be one hell of a long wait. So I walked back to the car and sat. Waiting.

How long it was before I saw her drive up to the apartment in a large convertible, I don't really know. I was thinking out my problem, trying to make sense out of it. But nothing had done any good. So I had finally given up and settled back, half-dozing with both eyes wide open.

She slowly parked her car and then walked into the apartment.

I decided to wait for a little while, to give her a chance to settle down. Then I'd strike. With plenty of questions. And no sex this time!

I smoked a cigarette and finally got out of the car, walked across the street, into the building and up to her apartment. I was determined to be sure that there wasn't any fooling around. What had happened before had been the most ridiculous thing that had ever happened to me. I'd had pick-ups throw themselves at me—but Betty had been something different.

I knocked on Betty Waters' door and then waited. For a while only silence answered me and then finally I heard the sound of footsteps and then the door opened.

Betty's face looked out at me, gaining a curious expression to it. She finally smiled.

"Why don't you come in?" she suggested.

I walked in and closed the door behind me. My first shock came when looking real close at Betty. She was wearing a loose-fitting negligee. Filmy and blue. It showed off just about every part of her voluptuous figure.

"Who're you expecting?" I asked.

She laughed throatily and then stepped back into the room.

"What do I owe this visit to?" she asked, sitting down on a sofa and stretching her body out in as sexy a way as possible.

"More of the same...?" Her voice drifted as her eyes swept my frame with eager and open invitation.

"Not quite, sister!" I snapped back, determined to fan the anger in me into a roaring flame so that she wouldn't have any chance, in the world, to excite my sexual desires again.

"Then what do I owe the pleasure of this visit to?" she inquired, half with her lips and half with the raising of her eyebrows.

"Let's say for a little questioning."

She smiled. "Oh, is that it?" Her voice held all of the innocence that her face expressed, but it was a false attitude. "Again?"

"Just what are your connections with Jack Leiver?"

She just smiled for a moment, looking up at me with her large eyes.

"And what did you bring me over to your apartment for the other day?" Questions were popping into my mind faster than I could express them in words. It was as if the answers didn't matter as much as voicing the questions to somebody—anybody! I forced myself to become calmer. Emotional response to the questioning wouldn't help me get anywhere!

"Sex?" she suggested.

"Come off it. There was a good reason. Leiver put you up to it?"

"How'd you guess?" she inquired. Her voice held all the angry contempt she could possibly get into it.

"Why?"

88

"You're smart; why don't you figure it out for your-self?"

"Why?" I repeated.

Silence.

"What is everybody after me for?" I asked.

Silence. She sat there looking across at me in that superior cocky way. Her eyebrows arched, not saying a word.

Her body was half stretched out on the sofa. Her breasts were large, round and inviting. She was a sight that could drive any man mad.

And I was mad—but in a different way, right then.

Ralph Pentron had been killed because of this woman. Or at least that was what everybody wanted me and everyone else to think!

That was a thought that had been bothering my subconscious mind for some time.

"Why was Ralph killed? And don't give me that crap about it being for you."

"But it was!"

"That's a lie!"

"Prove it!"

"I mean to."

Suddenly my breathing was getting shorter and heavier. I didn't know for sure that it was only from anger, either. My body was reacting to that beautiful sexy form before me, even though my mind was fighting with every ounce of strength against the reaction.

"Pentron was working for the police!" I blurted out.

Her expression changed only for a moment and then returned to the taunting look.

"So—he was working for Jack, too..." Her face changed to a worried frown as she broke off.

This was enough to drive my mind into full power. One needs something to hang their hat on. This just might be the hooker.

SOFTLY AS I KILL YOU, BY CHARLES NUETZEL

☛Chapter Eighteen☚

So that was it. He'd been working for both sides and been caught in the act. Couldn't go to the police without getting into trouble.

But did that really fit? That's what I had to find out. It didn't fit exactly. There were odd ends missing.

"So it was that?" I asked.

"I didn't say anything!" She had a worried expression on her face now, and for a while it looked like the tables had been dumped upside down; I had her going.

Stepping to the sofa I looked threateningly down at her. "Why'd you kill him? Acting like you were on his side?"

"I didn't kill him!" she screamed.

"It was just the same thing. You set him up."

"I had no choice!"

"Why?"

"Leiver would have killed me."

"Then he's using you!"

She just nodded, biting her lower lip. Her eyes looked down at the floor. "Ralph was a nice guy. The only man who had liked me for what I was—regardless of the things I'd...done in the past. He didn't care. He told me that he wasn't interested in what had happened to me before he met me. What counted was the way I acted now—"

"So you set him up for a kill," I cut in bitterly.

She just nodded, not saying anything.

I couldn't feel sorry for her. She'd sold out the only man who had probably ever really loved her. Sold out to save a pound of whoring female flesh that wasn't worth the price it cost.

I reached down and angrily grabbed hold of her shoulders, jerking her to a standing position. This was the time to follow through, even if it meant getting rough. The important thing was to push back and push hard while I had control of things.

"What does Leiver think I know about him? Why is he...afraid of me?"

She laughed in my face. It sounded slightly hysterical. "Afraid of you? That's a gas! He could stamp you out like an ant. You're nothing to him. Nothing at all!"

"Then why all the trouble with me? Wouldn't it be easier to just rub me out?"

"Don't think that he hasn't thought of that!"

"Then why not?"

"Because he just isn't that kind of man!"

Now that was a laugh. He kills Ralph—but he's just not that kind of man! "Then why did he kill Ralph?"

I squeezed her shoulders and she winced from the pain. "You...you're hurting...hurting me!" she sobbed.

"Tell me another sad story. Answer the question!"

"I don't know!"

"But he's not that kind of man?"

"He had a good reason. That's all I know!"

"You're lying!"

She suddenly smiled. That's when I remembered her reaction to pain the other day when I'd hit her. She'd liked it. She loved it.

My hands opened and fell to my side. "Okay. So pushing you around won't get me anyplace..." I sighed heavily, looking at her lovely body, all but unable to resist the urge to take it in my arms and crush the holy hell out of it. Well, crush is the wrong word. Ram the hell out of her.

She noticed the direction of my gaze and smiled. "What's wrong, lover-boy? Do you want me again? Like before?"

Words choked in my throat. There was something about this woman that was overpowering to a man. You couldn't really ignore her sexual appeal. She was a nympho. There was no doubt about that. Why would a woman dress like she was when she was alone? That had been my own experience with her. What kind of woman would offer herself to a total stranger like she had done?

I couldn't get my eyes or mind off her body for a few moments and she realized it, making the most of it.

"What do you want?" she demanded, opening the lacy-blue netting. "Come on, lover-boy."

I gulped, unable to do anything but stand there helpless.

"Come on, lover-boy, take what you really came here for!"

Desperately I did the only thing that I could. I doubled up my fist and swung.

The contact was perfect. It connected with her jaw. She went out. Just in time I caught hold of her, keeping her body from falling to the floor.

For a moment, as her form was against mine, I found it almost impossible not to make the hell out of it right then, regardless of the fact that she was quite unconscious. That was the way she affected me. Even then, I held her closer for a long delightful moment. Sighing heavily, I picked her up and carried her to the sofa and lay her down. I didn't dare look at her for fear of taking her instantly.

I was still breathing heavily when I moved from the sofa and started doing the only thing left for me to do; search her place for any evidence that might lead me to some of the answers, or to Jack Leiver.

Suddenly I realized this was an important element in the case. This piece had to be fit in and work out completely.

Jack Leiver.

What new insights would be revealed then?

Or was I running up another blind alley?

Long experience in this business has taught me that there can be all-too many bad leads. That's what makes it so blasted hard.

You think you have something hot and it turns cold even before you touch it.

But one thing for sure: This was a place to start.

Again.

SOFTLY AS I KILL YOU, BY CHARLES NUETZEL

☛Chapter Nineteen☚

It was thirty minutes later that I returned to my car and started in the general direction of central Los Angeles, to the place where I expected to find Jack Leiver.

Betty Waters had remained knocked cold for quite a while, and when she'd finally come out of it, she left me completely alone. And that was some comfort. We had reached a stage in the game where she didn't seem to want anything more to do with me. The only conclusion I could reach was that she didn't like being whacked on the jaw. She might dig a little batting around—that probably sexed her up a little—but she wasn't keen on the Sunday out-for-the-count haymaker! That was great!

I'd left her just as much alone. When I'd found what looked like the information I needed, I got the hell out as fast as I could.

One of the things I'd discovered before she'd come around and back to life had been an un-cashed paycheck made out to Betty Waters. It had been from a nightclub on Sunset. Later, I'd found the address of Jack Leiver. It was written on a piece of paper. Almost too nicely placed: like Betty Waters' name and address had been placed in Ralph Pentron's apartment for me to find.

I arrived at the address where Jack Leiver should be located, about twenty minutes after leaving Betty's place.

It was a large, old-fashioned apartment house. Built some time during the turn of the century, from the way it looked. Old and weathered. A good place for a hideout. So now I'd managed to find it, but I suddenly wondered what I planned on doing.

I could do like some mystery novel hero and barge in

95

with gun in hand and fists clenched tightly, hammering my way through a whole goddamned goon squad!

That wasn't me. But I did plan on doing the only thing that was open to me. Walk up and knock on the door of his place; when it was opened, ask to see Jack Leiver and then play it by ear from then on.

It was simply a case of having to do something—anything! Of course it was possible to just drop the whole matter.

But, again, that isn't me. If I get pushed around, have a murder rap shoved on top of me and then also have a good friend killed in the process, well, that's not me to back out. Under any circumstances!

I'm no hero, but I'm not a coward either. When something has been done to me, I'll do it back—regardless! I knew that I was walking into the lion's mouth, without any information as to what I was looking for. I couldn't come right out and say, "I want to turn you in, Mr. Leiver, for the murder of Ralph Pentron.' That wouldn't get me anywhere. Exactly what I expected to find I had no way of knowing.

I walked to the apartment. Read which room Jack Leiver had. I half expected it not to be listed outright. But it was. J-a-c-k L-e-i-v-e-r.

Suddenly a thought struck me; something that I'd forgotten about. Something that Bill Davidson had said to me. It had to do with Jack Leiver being connected with something big. I was to keep my hands off because this was BIG Government Business—That they had been after Leiver for a long time. That meant that Leiver was a big-time opera-tor—a behind-the-scenes man, maybe.

Then why such a crummy place?

So I knocked at the door marked 4-E, which had Leiver's name on it.

At first nobody answered and I had the sickening feeling that I was up a blind alley again.

Then the door opened.

The man who had been to my apartment that first day and shoved me around and later beaten me up was standing there looking out at me.

He smiled when he recognized who I was. "Well,

well, what have we here?"

He didn't move to open the door any wider. I moved forward. "Came to see Leiver!" I snapped, trying to push past him.

He refused to move. "What about?"

"None of your damned business!" I cursed, swinging at him before he had a chance to really get ready for my forward attack. The desire to kill was strong. The only thing was that he was more than ready. He moved like a trained prizefighter. My swing missed, but his didn't, it connected on the side of my face.

"Don't try that again, buster!" he snapped, grabbing hold of my arm and pulling me forward into the room. He closed the door behind me. "We've been expecting you, mister big time tough boy!"

He laughed as he tried to push me forward. But I didn't push. This time I did connect a direct swing into the man's jaw.

He shot across the room, an amazed expression on his face. Then he tripped over a small table and fell to the floor. For a moment I thought that he was going to flash out of the picture, but instead he struggled to his feet and came rushing toward me. His eyes were filled with red-burning hatred and fury.

Like I said, I'm no hero and I'm no coward. But the chips were stacked against me this time. There was only one thing to do. I pulled my gun out from under my shoulder holster and pointed it in his direction.

I never saw a face go so white so fast. He froze. His eyes widened and his lips turned white rimmed. "Don't do nothing fancy, mister."

"Just keep frozen and nothing will happen—buster!"

A voice from behind me cooled things down very quickly. "You can drop your gun, Mr. Benton."

Now that's the kind of line one just loves to hear.

When in trouble, get in deeper trouble.

I stood there for a moment trying to force myself to have the guts to do just anything *but* drop my gun.

The odds were against me.

Under such circumstances, death stares you right in

97

the eyes, right between them, and says,

"Buster, you better play it cool or this might be your very last chance!"

Playing it cool can mean moving fast, work for the switch, play for time or simply give up and die if that's what's in the offering.

Dying didn't seem the best of all answers.

Playing for time seemed the safe way to act out the next moments. A little praying wasn't beyond me, either.

Yet I still hesitated giving up the only item that might have any chance of saving my life—if that was what the odds were.

A gun in hand is better than ten thousand on the floor. If you are going to be shot at you might as well have a chance, at least, to shoot back.

Thus I faced the impossible dream. Dream?

Nightmare was more like it!

☛Chapter Twenty☚

I turned, feeling a sickness settle inside my gut. What might happen after I'd dumped my gun would not be as pleasant as getting shot right then and there. I turned and looked at the man.

He was tall and good-looking; black curly hair, even eyes slightly deep-set, an angular jaw. His lips were thin, but not really cruel looking—just careful, I didn't have to be told that this was Jack Leiver. It stuck out all over. He was dressed in at least a two-hundred-dollar suit. He smelled of the rot of the underworld. The look in his eyes, the half-crooked smile on his lips. And his empty hands.

And his empty hands!

His empty hands!

His hands were empty. He didn't have a thing in them. It had been a bluff and I'd fallen right into it.

All this had taken but a split second. Just time enough for me to let my eyes sweep the man.

And the moment I realized I'd been tricked I turned as fast as I could toward this first guy.

But it was too late. Before I could do anything the goon whipped me around, giving out a jab in my gut and spinning me off my feet. The next thing I knew I was lying on the floor and the big goon was standing over me, pointing my own gun at my face.

"Well, well, so now the thing has all turned around, back to where it belongs!" The man leered nastily at me, his eyes dark and brooding, but his smile filled with evil victory.

"That'll do, Bert!"

"But, boss—"

"I said to chop it, and I meant it!" Leiver stepped into

my line of vision, looking pleasantly down at me. "Well, I was wondering when you would come around to pay me a visit?"

I glared up at him, wanting to wipe that superior grin off his face. But there wasn't any chance of even getting close to doing that with the 'goon' standing by.

"Why don't you get up?" Leiver suggested, extending his hand.

I ignored the offered hand and picked myself up from the floor.

"Okay, Bert, you can go now," Leiver announced, half turning toward his goon.

That one surprised me, because it was the last thing one would have thought a man like Leiver would do under such circumstances. It took me aback slightly.

"What's the bit?" I asked rather foolishly.

Leiver looked at me for a long time, in silence, after his muscle man had left.

"Have a seat," he suggested with his whole arm. "Want a drink?"

"This is just too cozy for words!" I commented sarcastically, seating myself.

"Not really." He turned to look at me, his eyes deep and thoughtful. After a moment he asked: "Want that drink?"

I could have used one right then, but I was determined not to let him do me any favors—even to giving me a drink. I just shook my head.

"What kind of game are we playing now?" I asked, lighting a cigarette.

He didn't answer me at first, just taking his time fixing a highball. Then slowly he turned toward me, a strange amused expression on his face. "I believe that this is your play, Mister Benton."

"Okay, then," I said as pleasantly as possible, blowing smoke into the air. "Tell me what this whole thing is about!"

"What?" His arms raised in the air, helplessly.

"You know damned well. The killing of Pentron. Pushing the blame on me. Sending sex-machine after me. Why?"

100

His expression changed to a deadly serious one. "I think that this is all my business—not yours!"

I stood, looking angrily at him. "Look, I've just had about enough of this whole damned thing. All the crap!"

He just smiled thinly.

"I'm going to blow this whole thing into a million pieces!"

"What?" he exclaimed.

"You know damned well what I mean. You killed Ralph Pentron!"

"Prove it!"

"That shouldn't be too hard!"

"I don't know about that, Mr. Benton. The police believe that you did it."

"Oh, come off it!"

"Sure. They have all the evidence that they need. They found the body with you in the room. The gun had your fingerprints on it, etc. Got me?"

"Okay, Mr. Leiver, buster! So you made a frame-up job of it! So you think you can get away with it. So—"

"I did get away with it. And nobody—but nobody—can touch me! Got that?"

I stood there glaring at him, my breath coming in deep heavy gasps. Suddenly I was furious. What were we doing here, talking more or less calmly? What angle was he playing? What game? And where did I fit in? Why? Why had I been brought into the whole thing in the first place?

"Do you mind sitting down for a moment, my friend?" Leiver calmly demanded. His face was all seriousness. "I have a few things to tell you."

"Exactly what?"

"Sit!" He jabbed the air with his whole arm.

Slowly I sat down. Not because I was afraid of him, but rather because I wanted to hear what he might have to say.

He took his time, sipping from his drink. Then he looked directly at me. "What you came here for was to get information. Well, you've become too much of a headache. I guess I might as well tell you a little bit. It won't do you any good, because you won't be able to prove a thing!" He

sighed heavily and then continued. "Let's start with Ralph
Pentron. He worked for the government—"

"That doesn't really make sense. He had all the—"

"Money he wanted. Okay, let's say it was a hobby.
Well, then—where was I? Oh, yes. Pentron was pretty much
of a fool. I had been sent up for a year, and while I was playing out the term, he played up to Betty. The only thing was
that he didn't realize that I'd set Betty on him. For two reasons. She needs sex like normal people need air. I wanted to
know where she was and with whom. I also wanted to know
what Pentron's game was. I'd never been caught on anything
before. Only when Pentron started working for me did any
trouble start.

"Nothing had gone right. I got word from my police
contacts that there was a Fed agent in my crowd. So I put
two and two together and, being a careful man, set Betty Waters on him. I don't like killing unless it's completely necessary. Murder is a messy business. Especially in the racket
I'm in."

"Why you telling me this?"

"You'll find out in a little while, my nosy friend," he
sneered. Then he continued: "So when I pulled a few strings
with the big boys and got myself out of the pen, I went and
did what was necessary to keep Pentron quiet."

"Murder!"

"Let's call it a necessary action, caused by Ralph
Pentron's bit fat nose!"

He remained silent for a moment, sipping his drink
carefully. Finally he took a deep breath and said, "You happened to be around, so I fixed it up so that it looked like you
had done the job.

The only trouble with the frame was that we couldn't
get you on any solid motive. So you got off. We tried to keep
your nose out of this business. I put Betty Waters on you to
see if you knew anything. We searched your apartment to see
if there was anything there that might give us any idea of
what you might have known. You see, we didn't know if
Ralph Pentron told you anything about us."

"He didn't have time!"

I suddenly was aware that what he was telling me

was either a lie, or he wasn't saying all there was to say. Why hadn't Ralph gone to the police or his superiors, instead of calling me? I decided to leave the question unasked.

"That's all we wanted to know. But we figured that all out before this. That is, before you came here today."

"Just what kind of a racket are you in?"

He looked at me for a long time and then looked down at his drink. "I see you aren't about to keep out of my way, are you?" He didn't wait for the answer.

"But then, that's why I've been telling you all this. The only way I can justify killing you is to create a good reason. Tell you all, and then I couldn't let you live!"

He let that sink in.

It sank!

"You see, you aren't going to live past this hour!"

I jolted upright, glaring at him. "And who's going to stop me?"

"Bert!" he called.

His goon stepped in. There were three other men with him. All of them had guns in their hands.

"You can take this guy out for a ride. Dump him someplace!"

"Hey—wait a minute!" I yelled, desperately trying to stall for time. I didn't plan on being dead without a fight.

"You might tell me why I'm being..."

"Killed?"

"That's just about it. It won't hurt you none."

"Okay. Why not? You have a nose—why not fill it! We're in the simple racket of bringing narcotics into the country! That's all! We're awaiting a large shipment, now." He turned to his goon squad. "Okay—get rid of him!"

With that he walked out of the room, leaving me with the four men who had their guns pointed in my direction.

☞Chapter Twenty-One☜

I can't say that things looked particularly good for me at that moment. In fact, to put it bluntly, there didn't seem any way out.

I had the information I wanted. Not the proof. And not the answers—really. There was more to what he had told me than he'd been willing to admit. Something didn't figure in the jigsaw puzzle. But that didn't matter. As far as Jack Leiver was concerned I knew enough to let me be killed.

Betty Waters had been right about one thing:

Jack Leiver wasn't that kind of guy! He wouldn't kill somebody without a good reason—even if he had to create the reason!

I looked at the four goons and sighed. "I guess there's no way of talking you guys out of this?" I commented breezily.

"A comic!" The man named Bert just smiled at me. "What do you think, buster?"

Another man motioned to me with his gun. "This way!"

This way meant out the back door. I did as ordered, being roughly helped by Bert as I moved past him. He shoved me forward with a hard, powerful open hand.

"Where're you guys going to take me?" I inquired, trying to keep the shakes out of my voice. I'd be a liar if I said I wasn't scared. I'd be a fool not to be frightened.

"You should have kept your nose out of this whole thing—then maybe you'd live to see the next day!"

"I'm not dead yet!" I pointed out breezily.

The line was rewarded with a slap across the back of my head. That would be Bert! I thought. Well, one thing I was determined about—I wouldn't go out without a fight. Even if they did have the guns. They were going to kill me anyway, so I didn't have anything to lose. If I fought, at least I'd know that maybe one or two of these happy fellows would know that they'd killed a man and not a boy. I don't believe in giving in without a fight.

They moved me through the apartment and out to the back porch. There was a car in the driveway. They pushed me toward it.

Without warning or breaking stride, I twisted toward the man closest to me, swung a fist into the pit of his stomach and at the same time jerked the gun from his numb hand. It all happened in a fraction of a split second. No time to think what was happening or what I planned on doing. Only react and action. Move without thought or plan. Play it ad-lib.

I rammed the gun into his gut and pulled the trigger. Then I pushed him toward the other three.

The attack had come so fast that they were caught by surprise. I followed the first surprise with another surprise. I aimed and fired at the man named Bert. He twisted around and staggered for a moment. His gun went off, the bullet just missing my head by inches.

I fired at the other two men. My first shot went between them and my second went into the arm of the one on my left. By this time Bert had recovered from the shock of the minor wound I'd delivered to him and he started firing on me. His first bullet missed and the second one hit me right in the chest, just as I placed a perfect hole in the forehead of the fourth man.

I turned to face Bert, the world spinning around me, my vision blurring. The very air seemed to weigh in on me. I couldn't think for a moment. Everything was going blank. I pulled the trigger twice. Nothing happened after the first shot. My gun was empty. But that didn't bother me any more because the world jumped out of existence all at once.

I was dead!

That was the first reaction. I must be dead. What had happened...?

My thoughts started drifting through a black sea of

mud. It was hard to organize them.

Ralph was dead...Betty Waters and her big boobs...Jack Leiver...I was dead... But I couldn't be dead! If I was dead, then why had I...why was I thinking? Heaven? No! Hell!

A light was floating above my head. I couldn't focus on it. I couldn't keep it from weaving from left to right.

I felt sick.

Something was burning in my chest and I wanted to scream. The pain hurt.

Then blackness again.

The world spun madly. I felt sick again. Nothing made sense. I realized that I was alive. That was the only logical thing. Light popped before my eyes.

A man was leaning over me, looking down at my face.

"He's going to be all right," a voice said. I realized that it was the man speaking to someone else. I couldn't see who it was.

I tried to sit up but forceful hands held me down. "Just take it easy, son. You had a rough one. A real rough one!"

I tried to speak but nothing happened. Then I heard a woman's voice, but couldn't make out the words or who it was that had spoken.

The man said: "I'll give him a shot!" Then I felt a little pin prickle in my arm. The room spun and stopped existing.

How long I was out I don't know. The world came into focus every now and then, but I couldn't really remember what took place, even as it was taking place.

It was a dream world that didn't really exist at all.

Then I began having real life-type dreams. I saw Sherry Thomas, lying on a bed, completely nude. She called me over with her arms. Her whole body arched upwards; shivered, convulsively and then suddenly I was lying against her.

She vanished abruptly.

I was looking up into Sherry Thomas' face...

At first I thought it was a dream. Then I realized that

this was the real thing. But then she faded out as my eyes closed. I tried to open them, but couldn't.

Then the next thing I knew was that the doctor was leaning over me.

"You look pretty good for what you went through. In another week you should be up and around."

My mind screamed: a week!

Good God, I had to get up and round up Jack Leiver!

"I gotta get up!" I said weakly.

The doctor laughed. "Not on your life. You're to stay in bed for some time."

The voice faded and the world became calm again. I didn't dream much, but had the feeling of unrest. Something was bothering my subconscious mind and I couldn't figure out what it was.

Something was wrong. Terribly wrong.

I struggled with my thoughts in the dazed nightmare condition that my mind was in, but it didn't do any good. It was like trying to think when you're asleep—which was exactly what I was trying to do—the only thing was that I didn't realize what or where I was.

I had no sense of identification. Nothing seemed real. And I tried desperately to make sense out of everything. But nothing happened. Nothing made sense.

Finally light came into focus again.

This time it had more solid shape.

The first thought was that I should be dead. Then the next thought was an attempt to figure out why I wasn't dead. After that I tried to understand where I was.

A hospital.

But which one?

How'd I gotten there?

The last thing I remember before...

Before what?

I couldn't think logically for a long time and then finally I managed to weed out the dream world from the real world. At least enough to remember the last thing that had happened before I'd landed wherever I was now.

Jack Leiver had ordered his men to kill me. Then there had been the fight. I'd shot up a few men and then been...shot!

Shot! Then why was I still alive?

I should be at the bottom of some river or the ocean. I should be dead!

There was one of those small buzzers that all hospitals have at the sides of the beds. I rang it.

I had to get some answers—and now.

☛Chapter Twenty-Two☚

It was only a few minutes before the nurse came into my room. "Let me see the doctor!" I demanded.

"Oh, Mr. Benton, I see you're awake. How are we feeling?"

Why doctors and nurses always ask how "we" are feeling is something that will probably remain unanswered for as long as they continue to exist.

"We are feeling good enough to get the hell out of this damned place!" I fairly shouted.

She looked shocked for a moment and then she smiled. "But you can't leave."

"Oh, can't I?" I demanded, starting to raise myself from the bed. A pain jabbed through me and I felt suddenly weak and dizzy.

"See what I mean? I'll go get the doctor. I think he'll want to see you, now that you're up. I mean, awake."

She left.

I waited, fighting the nausea and dizziness. I had to get up and moving. I had to have questions answered.

It seemed forever before she returned with the man whom I recognized as the doctor who'd been in my "nightmares."

"Hello, young man," he said. "I'm Doctor Smith. How are we feeling?"

There we go again, I thought bitterly. "I don't know how you're feeling, doc, but I've got to get out of here!"

"Now, now. I don't think that will be at all possible. You've gone through quite a bit. You almost died." All the time he spoke he was beginning to examine me with his fingers. Then he went right into the real one-two, taking my

111

pulse and blood pressure. I let him have his wild way, while trying to organize my questions in my mind. Finally I started with the third degree.

"Where's... I mean, how'd I get here?"

"You were found on the highway."

"What?"

"Outside the...in the valley. Whoever did this to you must have thought you were really done for. You almost were."

"Anything else?"

"I think the police will want to question you. And a Mr. Davidson has been calling daily."

"Daily?"

"Every day you've been here."

"How long?"

"A little over a week."

I felt suddenly sick inside. Days shot to hell. But then, what was the big rush?

Yet for some reason I couldn't help feeling that the time wasted had been valuable.

"What about Sherry?" I asked.

"Miss Thomas?"

"It seems to me that I...well, remember seeing...her."

"She was here. Every day. That girl is very much concerned."

"My secretary. Probably worried that if I die she has to go out and get another job..."

The doctor shook his head from side to side, smiling sadly at me. "I think it goes deeper than that."

I let that ride. I didn't like the idea of some romantic interest-taking place between Sherry and myself. That is—no serious interests. Well, okay. I was somewhat uncertain and confused about that.

"I think you'd better stay around for a few days more."

I looked at the doctor for a long moment and then sighed. "Isn't there anything else...I mean, can't I get out sooner? It's important!"

He shook his head.

"Then get me Bill Davidson!"

He looked oddly at me. "Right now?"

"Right now! It's important. Believe me—time is wasting. If I can't get out, then you'd better help me. Get Davidson!"

"Okay, anything you say. Nurse, give him a..." I didn't hear the rest because he spoke in such a low whisper.

Then both of them turned and left. A few moments later the nurse returned, smiling. "This will make us feel better..." she announced, jabbing my arm with a needle.

It made me feel better, all right. It blacked out all awareness. Nothing!

Blackness. No conscious dreaming.

Time wasted.

The next thing I remember is opening my eyes and looking up into the eyes of Dr. Smith. "You have a visitor here, Mr. Benton," he said, moving aside.

Bill Davidson was standing at the bedside looking down at me. "I see you finally made it around. Been waiting for several hours. What'd you want to see me about?"

For a moment I just looked at the lawyer and then nodded to the doctor and his nurse who was standing beside him. "Get these people out of here, first!"

The two left and Davidson pulled a chair over close to the bed. "Well, shoot!"

Then, slowly and with effort, I began to explain what Leiver had told me. Everything. And the fact that Leiver was responsible for what had happened to me.

When I had finished, Davidson just nodded. "Anything else?"

"Anything else?" I demanded, shocked. "What else do you *want?* "

"Something concrete!" was his professional, hard-line retort.

I lay there just looking up at him in stunned silence. He was supposed to be my friend.

"Look, Dan. You haven't told me anything the police could do anything with!" The expression in his eyes was almost pleading—though not desperate.

"You mean to tell me that he ordered me rubbed out because I knew exactly *nothing* of value?" That didn't make

113

sense. It sounded like a nightmare.

"That's exactly what he did!" was his stunning reply.

"Then..." I asked slowly, almost to myself, "Where do I go from here?"

But I knew the answer already. Davidson's answer wasn't required.

"From the top, I'd imagine."

I felt like giving him a nice fat "Thanks for nothing," but let it lay there to rot in silence. Some better answer had to come up.

And considering my physical condition I'd have plenty of time to come up with a lot of mental activity before going back out into the world of harsh reality.

Somewhere in my subconscious mind was the feeling I'd missed something important. If it surfaced, maybe I could start from the middle and work outwards until the solution revealed itself.

When Davidson left, my mind began its slow, torturous inner mental journey to somehow find a few subtle "missing" parts.

Something had to make sense out of all this.

But what?

☛Chapter Twenty-Three☚

In the next few days as I lay there in the bed, I had a lot of time to think things over. Things had slipped my mind during the last frantic days of running around chasing my tail for no good effects. All I'd managed to do was get myself banged around, beaten up and almost killed by Jack Leiver. And thinking about it, it all seemed fantastic. What purpose? What reason?

One thing that I finally came to a conclusion about: I'd have to start right at the beginning again and run through the whole thing.

The problem, when it was broken down to the simple elements, was Ralph Pentron. He'd had been killed for an unknown reason. For another unknown reason, the blame had been shifted onto me.

Maybe I was putting too much importance on the blame being shifted to me. Maybe if I reversed it. Why had I been released from jail? No motive. Everybody said that. Leiver. Davidson.

Suddenly I was beginning to wonder if they weren't working together. But that didn't make sense.

Yet both of them had tried to keep my nose out of the whole affair. All for different reasons.

Leiver, because he was afraid of what I might find out. Davidson, because he said it was government business. Then Larson had given me the push around with a quiet ride to jail.

Suddenly I remembered something about what Leiver had said. Something about his "contact" in the police department having told him that there was a Fed in his organization.

That thought jolted me. Who could be giving him information about such matters?

Larson?

That was insane. The thought almost made me laugh. Larson was as honest as they come. And there were hundreds of people who might give information. Maybe some rookie—some clerk. A police reporter.

That thought struck me suddenly numb. It might explain why Ralph had been afraid to go to the police.

There was plenty of time to think about the whole thing. And I used it as best I could.

Several times while I was in the hospital I had Sherry in to check up on a few things for me. Things that had to be checked. Like: when had Ralph last worked with a band? She discovered that he'd been fired because he'd been using narcotics.

That was a surprise that jarred me completely. One didn't expect to find that a good friend had been on the dope kick, especially when he had as much money as Ralph had.

Suddenly things started to work together a little.

And finally the doctor gave me the okay to get out of the hospital.

The first stop was Betty Waters' place!

Only thing, she wasn't there. It was late in the evening when I finally arrived, pulling my car up to the front of her apartment.

My first reaction was depression. Where could she be? This time of night she should be...

At work!

I suddenly remembered that she worked at a club on the Sunset Strip.

Going back to my car I started the engine and headed to that nightspot.

That's where I was going to find her—I felt sure of it! The moment I stepped into the place I spotted her. She was working as a cocktail waitress. She had on one of those tight-fitting, low-cut black jobs that dipped down so much at the front that it almost wasn't there at all.

Stepping up to the bar and sitting on a chair next to the place where the cocktail waitress comes to get her orders,

I waited until she stepped up.

At first she didn't notice me. But when she did, her face went deathly white. As if she were seeing a dead man.

SOFTLY AS I KILL YOU, BY CHARLES NUETZEL

☛Chapter Twenty-Four☚

That first reaction on her face shocked me just as much as I must have shocked her; then I realized that she, no doubt, thought I was dead.

For a moment I believed she would faint, but she finally gained control of herself and then leaned closer, whispering in a half choking voice. "What do...do you...want?"

I stared at her for a long time and finally answered: "To see you!"

She didn't say anything for a second, her eyes deep in thought.

"You—you're supposed to be dead!" she whispered.

"Thanks," I snapped back, "Take a break, now, or I'll start pulling a few capers on my own that will shove you right where you belong!"

She shook her head.

"I...I can't!" she choked out, frantically.

"Want to go to the police?"

Her head slowly moved from side to side. Her eyes were wide with open fear.

"Please...please leave me alone!" she pleaded. "He'd...kill me!"

"That's your problem, sister!"

"I can't!" she cried out.

"So, I'll call the police!" I stood, but she grabbed hold of my arm, pulling me back.

"Okay...a few minutes."

Then she moved away and went into the back of the night club and disappeared.

I waited.

Nothing happened.

119

I waited for twenty minutes over two drinks before I realized what had taken place. Anger and disgust stabbed through me. She'd pulled one of the oldest tricks in the book on me and I'd fallen for it. She'd blasted the hell out of there like a woman chased by a ghost.

Angrily I ordered a third scotch on the rocks and downed it in one gulp. First stop would be her apartment. I didn't expect to find her there, but I'd have to try.

Fifteen minutes later I pulled up in front of her place. Killed the engine and jumped out of the car. A minute later I was banging on her door.

No answer. The only thing else to do was try breaking the damned door down. After the third time of smashing my shoulder into the wooden obstruction, it burst open, the hinges jerking off the doorframe. It took only a few seconds to discover that the apartment was empty.

When I walked out into the hallway there were several people looking at me. I just ignored them, rushing out of the place and to my car.

The second possibility was Jack Leiver's. That was across town. I cursed myself for not having gone there in the first place. She would have headed for him right off. But it was too late to do anything about that mistake except get to Leiver's as fast as possible.

It took a little over thirty minutes since traffic on the freeway was jammed because of an accident. When I pulled up to the building I felt my insides go cold. It looked like nobody was home. But I quickly slid out of the car and walked up to the place, pulling my revolver from its shoulder holster. This time I didn't plan on being caught unaware.

The place was as dark as death itself. Nothing was in it. I knocked, but no answer.

Replacing the gun as I walked to the apartment across the way, I knocked and waited for the door to be answered. Finally it swung open and a heavy, older woman looked out.

"Do you know when Mr. Leiver is expected back?" It was a foolish question, but the first thing that popped into my mind.

She looked at me for a long time and then announced: "Why, he's been out of there for several weeks—

ever since that horrible shooting."

I cringed inwardly, but managed to remain outwardly calm.

"What shooting?" I asked.

"Why...it was all in the newspapers. I saw, or rather heard, most of it. Who would know that right next door was a horrible gangster..." She shivered, then continued. "It all happened so fast that it was over before anybody called the police. Papers said a Mister Benton had been shot and three other killers. I saw it all. It was horrible. Just like television." Her voice got slightly excited sounding. "Mind you, I didn't see their faces. They shot it out just like they do on television. The one who was wounded took the man he'd killed and lifted him into the parked car and then drove him away, after another man—that Mr. Leiver that horrible... Oh!" Her voice caught in a terrified choke. Her hand went to her lips. "You...you must be one of his horrible—"

"No. No, lady. I'm...from the...police." Quickly I backed away, turned and walked from the place before she got more scared than she already was. I heard the door slam behind me.

A moment later I was behind the wheel of my car. I drove for a long time, not in any particular direction. Thoughts of confusion were racing through my brain. But one thing I had found out, something about what had happened after I'd hit the ground after the "shoot-out." The rest I could fairly well figure out for myself. Bert and Leiver had driven me out and dumped me in the first possible place they could find, and then they'd got the hell out.

That left me nowhere! Just exactly nowhere!

Finally I turned the car in the direction of my apartment. Then changed my mind. There wasn't anything that I could do now. I'd chased away my only possible contact— Betty Waters. Suddenly I was tired of everything. I needed a little solace and help. Sherry Thomas came to my mind first.

When a man is confused and all shook up and all beaten, there is nothing better than a woman. And Sherry would be the best thing I could turn to.

I arrived at her place about an hour later. Knocking on the door I nervously waited for her to answer.

Finally the door opened and she stood there, a strange expression on her face.

"Well, you're the last person in the world I expected to find here at my door step." For a moment she half smiled and then her attitude changed to slightly chilling.

"Well, aren't you going to invite me in?"

She seemed to think that over for a moment and then sighed. "Okay...come on in." She was acting as if she were doing me some favor.

She closed the door behind me.

Everything about the room was the same as it had been the many times I'd been there before. Everything about the room—but nothing about Sherry. It was as if she knew what I'd come for and she didn't seem to like it.

I ignored that. "How about a drink, baby?"

She shrugged, and the action made her dark hair flow around her creamy shoulders. She was delightfully attractive, but she had a sad look about her eyes.

"What's wrong?" I asked stupidly.

She looked at me sharply. "What in the world do you mean?"

I didn't answer that. Instead I moved across the room to the cabinet where I knew she kept her liquor supplies. "Mind if I help myself?" I asked, going ahead and doing just that, without waiting for her okay.

She sighed heavily, but didn't move from the spot where she stood.

"Want one?"

She didn't answer so I fixed a second whiskey highball. Stepping over to where she was stonily waiting, I handed Sherry the glass I'd fixed her.

"What's bugging you, baby?" I asked, walking to the sofa and sitting down. "Come on over and sit by me."

She shook her head and then after a moment of silent thought, biting her lower lip, she moved over and sat down beside me.

For a long while neither of us said anything. I was trying to decide what was the best way to approach her.

I needed Sherry. Physically. But I couldn't really reason out the logical answer. Maybe just because a man will go to a woman's arms when he's had enough. I'd had enough, suddenly. Run up against blank walls and gotten nowhere. There is just so much a man can take before he is just all done in. I'd had it, for the moment, anyway. And I needed Sherry's body to wipe away all the defeat.

She didn't move. It was as if she were frozen—or afraid to move or say anything.

I sipped my drink until there wasn't anything left in the glass. Sighing heavily I walked to the liquor cabinet and refilled my glass—this time with straight booze. I needed a good jolt and I planned on getting it. If not Sherry, then complete boozing escape.

Turning, I stood there for a long time just looking at Sherry. Taking in the lovely sweep of her body. She was dressed in a tight-fitting red dress. It showed off her figure without making any attempt to be sexy. But it was sexy, because Sherry was sexy. She had the kind of body that a man wanted more than once. She had something about her whole appearance that made a man desire more and more of her.

The more I looked at her the more I wanted her.

Finally I let my eyes move to her lips. They were half-parted and moist. Full and red. Soft and silky.

"What's with you, baby?" I finally managed to ask in much too husky a voice

She looked sharply at me Her eyes seemed moist, but heavy with some inner fury

"That's just it?" she snapped bitterly.

"What?" I cried in alarm. I didn't really expect such an outburst.

"Baby. Baby, baby, baby. Baby!" She half screamed out the words, her voice high and excited and angry. "Everybody's 'baby' to you. Every slut and whore. You don't know the difference between a real woman and one like that...that Miss Waters!" A choke had stopped her for a moment.

"What?" I cried in surprise. First anger flashed through me; then it left. And to my surprise there was something else. Something I couldn't believe. I realized what was bothering her. I'd been shoving it with Betty Waters—from the way she looked at it—and every other woman that came along, and then when the chips dropped I turned to Sherry. It was just a normal feminine reaction. And I suddenly realized that for some reason I felt sorry for her. More than that, I suddenly didn't particularly like myself.

"Oh, baby...Sherry. You...believe me!" I choked on my own words. There is a time for words and then there is a time for action. I realized that anything I might say right then wouldn't do any good.

Sherry felt that I'd been using her. It had never occurred to me that she would really care about such things. She'd always been such a ball— all the time. All for fun, but no questions asked. Now I realized that she wasn't like that at all.

She was like all other women, wanting a man to want her and nobody else. She wanted to feel that he really cared when he took her in his arms.

Looking at her now, I felt all the longing and emotion that a man does feel when he is near the woman that means more to him than any other. She was more than just a woman; more than a secretary; more than just a quick affair. Not that I was in love. Surely not that! Let's say that I felt a strongly tender affection toward Sherry, and the idea that she might feel emotionally hurt made me feel pretty damned low.

"Look, baby..." The words faded out. I'd taken a step in her direction. But I froze.

She was gazing up at me with a blank expression. Her whole body was rigid; not with coolness, but with something else. There was a look about her. The half parting of her lips. Suddenly I knew what I had to do—and it was exactly what I wanted to do.

Moving over to her I reached for Sherry and pulled her close. She only struggled for a moment, and then her body relaxed against mine.

Too many emotions were flooding through me, then, for any physical action to take place. I just held her for a long while. Aware of her body next to me. Her firm, full breasts breathing against my chest. Also there was something else I was abruptly aware of—she was silently sobbing.

God, what a bastard I was! I thought, bitterly.

"Sherry...Sherry..." I hardly heard her, "yes."

124

"I...I'm sorry..."

"I know."

"I'm a fool—"

"No...no... No! No, you aren't!" She pulled away slightly. Her eyes looked into mine. They were moist with tears. "No, darling... I'm the fool! You're a man...there're no strings attached between us. It's been for kicks. I can't help feeling the way I do toward you...after you...almost dying...and I worried so..."

I pulled her closer, cutting off her words with my lips.

That first kiss had all the tenderness of two lovers kissing for the first time. We held each other for a long while, without saying anything. I could feel her heart beating next to mine. It was one of those times when a man and woman aren't passionate, but rather tender and affectionate. I found, suddenly, that I had a deep inner need for Sherry. It couldn't be called love—but it was close enough.

All at once we were kissing again. But this time it was with our whole bodies. Her lips, parted and wide, biting against mine.

My arms circled her body and started working on the zipper of her dress.

She looked up at me, smiling. "This is...the only way a woman...should demand her man." Her voice was low and husky.

Then her arms reached up and pulled me down, down toward the throbbing white silk of her throat. I kissed it softly at first, just brushing my lips along its velvet surface.

She murmured in my ear: "I was a fool...you know that."

"Forget it. I'm just as much!"

"No...no. It's just that...well, I need you so."

"I need you, too, baby."

She cringed only slightly as I used the word "baby," but managed to smile, shrugging. "What else can I expect from a man like you? After all, you just aren't the type to settle down with a woman..."

When I awoke, next to Sherry, it was daylight.

For some reason I had a feeling of nervousness.

As if something was about to happen. A sense.

An inner awareness that had no logic. Then the phone rang.

Sherry sat up next to me.

"What is it?" she demanded sleepily.

"The phone. Answer it. I'm not here!" I don't know what made me say that, but something warned me to be careful.

Slowly Sherry got up and moved to the phone. She whispered "Hello" and then just stood there nodding and getting whiter and whiter. Finally she said, "I don't know where he is...yes, of course I'll call you the moment I hear from him."

Then she hung up and turned toward me. Her eyes were wide with horror, her white-rimmed. Hardly above a whisper announced: "The police are after you...for the murder of Betty Waters."

☛Chapter Twenty-Five☚

I couldn't believe what I heard. On two levels. Betty Waters was dead. The only possible connection to Jack Leiver. The only weak link. And I knew that he must have realized that too. Why else would he kill her?

Then, have the murder blamed on me. That didn't figure. I had to do something about that, and I didn't know exactly what, at first.

A long time passed before I said anything to Sherry. We both froze where we were, just looking at each other. At last I said: "Okay, now what? A hell of a note!"

She didn't say anything to that, but instead moved to my side and kissed my cheek. "You'll think of something." That was it. Something. Anything! "Call Davidson. See what he knows about it." She moved back to the phone and dialed Davidson's number. They talked for a long time and finally she hung up.

"They found her in your apartment, dead."

"Who found her?"

"Lieutenant Larson!"

That figured. Pretty much to the very end. Larson. The police "contact" which Leiver had mentioned. Well, that was a start. I couldn't get Larson at the police department, but it wouldn't be hard to find out where he lived. That would be start number one!

"See you later, baby," I told Sherry, as I got dressed.

"Where are you going?"

"To find Larson!"

"You can't do that. They'd arrest—"

"Not if I get him alone, they won't. Anyway, I have a score to settle with him!"

"No—" she cried, her hand going to her lips. "Don't do anything drastic!"

"Baby, this is...this calls for something drastic! They have me penned in from every side. There isn't anything else that I can do. I've been pushed around just as long as I intend to be pushed. Now I'm pushing back until either I fall for good or they fall for good!"

Moving to her side I pulled her tightly to me. For a long moment I held her and kissed her. I wanted to remember what it was like feeling her, just in case it was the last chance I got.

"I'll be back to continue matters—later!"

She didn't say anything to that, only patting me gently on the arm. She smiled weakly and then I turned and walked out of the apartment.

First stop was my place. That might be a trap, but it was where I kept my "little black book" with the listings of addresses—including Lieutenant Larson's home address. There wasn't any choice. His address had been hard to get and I didn't want to go through all that again. Time was against me. If necessary I could use force to search my own place.

I arrived half an hour later, but drove past the apartment house. It was swarming with people. Police and reporters. I'd have to wait.

Then I spotted Lieutenant Larson in the group of people walking out of the building. There he was, the man I wanted, and there wasn't any way of getting him—then. I drove on.

I had to kill time for over five hours, but finally the place looked pretty deserted. But it would have been a fool's play to just walk in the front way—they would have a cop waiting in the place for me, just in case I happened to show up.

Parking the car a block down the street I walked up to my apartment from the back way. I'd placed my revolver in my side pocket, where I kept my hand, ready for any possible emergency.

Up the back steps and down the hall. There wasn't anybody in the hallway. I had two choices: one was to barge in and make a swift play, and the other was simply to walk in and if somebody was there try to outsmart them. That was a gamble. Unlocking and opening the door, I stepped in.

"Hello," a voice greeted me.

I felt a sickening grind inside me. Action was the only thing that was left.

"What's this?" I asked, pulling my hand out of my pocket, with the revolver in it.

"Just stay where you are!" I demanded. There were two men in there waiting for me. They looked surprised.

"What you doing?" the one by the window demanded.

The other said, "This won't get you anywhere, Dan."

I recognized him then. I couldn't remember his name at first, but I knew we'd worked together for some time when I was on the force. That would explain their carelessness in letting me get the drop on them.

"Davidson sent us here."

That one left me cold. "Why?"

"He overrode Lieutenant Larson. Wanted us to bring you down to his office. If you happened to show up here."

"On what charge?"

"Don't be silly—you know what the score is."

"Yeah, a frame—that's it!"

"Come along with us—he'll see that you get every break in the world."

"But I didn't do it! That's all."

"Why the gun, then?"

"I have a few things to check out on my own."

The man by the window sighed. "I told you, Jim, that we should have gone after him like any other hood."

"Davidson said no guns. That Benton would come on in without any trouble."

"I hate to do this—but I'm not coming. There are too many things that have to be done—first." I felt like hell going against Davidson like this.

"Don't be a fool, Benton!"

"Tell Davidson I need just a little time. If I don't have what I'm after in twenty-four hours, I'll turn myself in to him."

The man shrugged. "You're playing a stupid game."

"No choice. Now you two move over to the wall— and don't try anything. As far as you're concerned, I've killed at least one person, and have nothing to lose by killing you!"

They both did as I told them and I went to my desk and opened the middle drawer. Taking out the book with the necessary addresses in it, I moved toward the cops. "Now I'll just take your guns." Doing that, I ordered them into the closet and closed the door. I put a chair under the knob, moved from the apartment and rushed outside to my car.

Pulling the car away from the curb I gunned it down the street, trying to get out of there sooner than the police could get a net around the area. It wouldn't be too long before the two cops would be out of the closet and calling all the patrol cars in the area to bring me in. This time they wouldn't be so nice about it; it would be a case of getting me any way that they could.

When I was several miles from my apartment I stopped the car on a side street and looked up Lieutenant Larson's address It was on the other side of town. I started the car and headed in that direction.

I drove past his place and parked the car half a block away. Close enough to be able to see the place, when Larson returned home.

I waited for several hours, smoking one cigarette after another. There was plenty of time to think, but nothing new occurred to me. The only thing that I could do was to play it by ear. And that was what I planned on doing.

Finally I was tired of waiting; my mouth was already raw from smoking too much. I got out of the car. There was only one way to move things faster. It looked like I'd have to wait for a long time before Larson returned home and I didn't like the idea of waiting too long. Time was the only thing that I didn't have much of.

Walking to the large house listed as Larson's, I moved up the walk and rang the doorbell.

It was some moments before the door opened. A middle-aged woman looked out. She had a tragic look about her. The lines in her face showed tiredness. The wrinkles around her sad eyes were worried.

"Yes?" she asked, sounding almost afraid.

"Is Lieutenant Larson in?"

She shook her head slowly from side to side.

"Well, I have to see him."

"He's down at the station."

"Can't go there!" I pushed forward before she could realize what I was doing, and stepped into the house.

"You...you can't come in here!"

"I've done it, lady!" I told her, forcing the door closed behind me

She looked at me in terror "Who are you?"

"Let s say I'm a friend of your husband's."

She thought that over for a moment and then sighed "I guess you re one of his gangster friends."

For a moment I felt sorry for her, but I kept the emotion from showing on my face. There was too much that depended on me being as forceful as possible—even if I had to scare the living hell out of her.

"When do you expect him back home?"

"About...six."

I looked at my watch. That was half an hour away. "Okay, then—I'll wait!"

I walked into the living room and sat down, making myself at home, trying to hold down the nervousness that was hammering in my gut. "You stay here, where I can keep an eye on you."

Her breath caught, then she stood straight, glaring at me. "I don't know who you are, but you can't tell me what to do in my own house!" She started to turn to leave.

I pulled the gun from my shoulder holster and pointed it at her.

"Just stay where you are!" I ordered.

She must have seen the gun in my hand out of the corner of her eye, for she turned back. She looked at me in horror for a moment, her mouth working nervously. Finally she moved across the room and sat down on the sofa.

We waited in silence. Waited for Lieutenant Larson to return home.

SOFTLY AS I KILL YOU, BY CHARLES NUETZEL

Seven minutes after six the front door opened and Larson walked in.

☛Chapter Twenty-Six☚

There was a long frozen silence as Larson saw me sitting in his living room. Then he made a movement toward the gun under his arm.

"I wouldn't do that, if I were you!" I ordered, showing him the point of my revolver, directed at the center of his stomach.

His hand froze.

"What are you doing here?" he demanded, looking frantically toward his wife. His eyes were narrowed, his lips drawn tightly across his teeth.

"What the hell are you doing here?" he asked again. I took my time answering, letting him suffer for a while. "Let's say I have a few questions to ask you."

Slowly his eyes widened slightly. I could easily see that he was more than just a little nervous. Then he moved across the room toward his wife.

"He hasn't harmed you, has he?" he asked in an almost tender voice.

She just shook her head from side to side, biting her lower lip. Then he turned and looked at me.

"I'll..." his voice broke off.

For a long while we stared at each other.

"Mind if I have a drink?" he asked me.

"Yes! Just stay where you are!"

"What you doing here? We've been looking all over for you—"

"And I've been waiting for you right here in your living room."

"Well, your time isn't for long!" he growled. "We'll get you!"

133

"Who? The police? Or you and your buddies?"

"What the hell are you talking about?" he gulped out, his eyes widening with surprise.

"Leiver and the boys!"

"What the hell?"

"Just that!" I let it sink in. "I want Leiver—and I know you're working for him!"

He didn't say a word, just stood there staring at me in confusion.

"Come on, Larson, you know and I know that you've been playing ball with those guys. That's why I've been getting into so much trouble.

"That's why Pentron wouldn't go to the police until he'd made sure he would be safe. That's why he called me up..." I was shooting blankly, but it had to be bluffed out. If I were right then he'd bend under the abrupt charges.

He didn't bend, and he didn't even get excited. Instead he only smiled across at me. "You have quite an imagination for a killer!"

His wife took in a breath of shocked fear, looking at me with terrified wide eyes.

"I don't think so. No imagination. Pentron told me everything, that morning." It was a bold-faced lie, but I only hoped that it would fool him.

It worked—only slightly, but enough to get a quick reaction. Confusion showed in his eyes. He narrowed them, and his mouth twitched slightly.

"You're a fool. And I'll personally see that you get the chair, Benton. The chair for killing Betty Waters!"

"Whose idea was that? Yours, or Leiver's? Oh, but it must have been Leiver's. You don't have the brains to think up such bright ideas. He's the mastermind in this racket."

"You're a dead man, Benton. Why don't you give up? This story telling won't get you anywhere."

"Oh, come on. You're a pretty good actor, Larson. But you don't fool me. Not even a little bit! I've had it up to there with you and your buddies," I countered, standing and walking over toward him. I took hold of his collar and pushed him into a chair. "Now I think it's about time we quit playing!"

134

"Don't hurt him!" his wife cried in alarm, her voice high and thin with emotion.

"Sister, nobody will hurt your husband except himself! All he has to do is say a few words, and I'll leave him alone!"

Larson looked up at me; his expression had a worried look about it.

"What you going to do?" he demanded in a voice that sounded like it was a bit on the shaky side.

"That depends on you. I want Leiver!"

"Why ask me? How would I know?"

"Don't give me that, asshole!"

"I don't know what you're talking about!" His eyes dropped from mine, his hands nervously working on the arms of the chair.

I put the barrel of my gun right between his eyes. "Are you going to stop playing games or do I have to use this?"

"You wouldn't dare!"

Pulling the gun away, I swung the back of my hand across his face. "Not right away, I wouldn't use it. First I'd give you a little working over. Then you'll beg for a hole in your head."

A sob of alarm sounded from his wife.

"Tell him!" she cried.

"Shut up!"

"If you don't tell him, I will!" she told her husband.

I turned toward her. "Okay, how about it?"

That was a mistake. Larson jumped without warning and knocked me over. I didn't have time to recover before he smashed a fist into my face and knocked the gun from my fingers. But by then I'd swung the side of my hand outwards toward his head. He slammed backwards, falling to the floor. Then I leaped for my gun, at the same time kicking out at Larson. My foot caught him in the gut and he rolled over, moaning.

I stood and looked down at him. After a while he sat up, glaring at me in terrible agony.

"Okay! About Leiver!" I ordered, keeping the gun pointed in his direction.

135

He gasped in pain and then after wiping his forehead with the back of his hand; he said: "He's...coming here, to-night. But you—you gotta get out of here! You don't under-stand—"

That was the last thing I heard. A numbing object hit the back of my head.

Lights out!

Finished.

I fell to the floor, black defeat clouding around my vision and awareness.

☙Chapter Twenty-Seven☙

First I was aware of voices. The next thing I was aware of was light.

"...What are you going to do with him?" Larson asked, his voice heavy with concern.

"Kill. Kill him for good, this time!" That was Leiver's voice. "We have everything we need now, and can get the hell out of here and head for New York as soon as the boss gets here. The boys there will pay plenty of money for the packet we've got. And plenty more for the information on how to get a lot more of it. This is big business. With Benton out of the way there's no way to put the squeeze play on us. We'll be free of all the big noses. The D.A. can't touch us. The murders won't be looked into after Benton-boy has written the confession I have in mind."

I heard a moan. At first I couldn't make out from what direction it had come. Then I realized that it had come from my own lips.

"Well, baby boy has come around!" a third voice announced.

I felt a slap sting across my face.

My eyes opened. I was looking directly into Bert's face. Leiver's goon squad.

At first impulse I surged upwards to strike at him, but he pushed me back. "Just stay where you are, buster-boy!"

For a moment I didn't move, and then after a while I looked around. Someone had placed me in a chair. From where I sat I could see everybody. Leiver, Larson, his wife, and goon-squad Bert.

"So, we meet again, my friend," Leiver greeted, moving toward me. "You've sure cost me a lot of trouble! But I believe that's just about over."

"Don't be too sure of that, asshole!" I snapped back.

"A wise guy," Bert commented, slapping me across the face,again. I hardly felt the blow. I was too mad to feel anything right then. I'd seen some rough times, but the cards seemed pretty well stacked against me now. I looked at the woman and said bitterly, "Nice going, Mrs. Larson—you've just helped your husband kill a man!"

She cringed at my words "What else could I do? He's my husband."

Women! That was a woman for you. Stick by a man who might be anything—even a killer or a crooked cop.

"Cut the chatter," Leiver ordered. "We have important business to take care of.

"Bring our friend over here to the desk," he told his goon squad.

Bert jerked me upright and shoved me forward. "Do as the man tells you."

"What now?" I asked, playing dumb. Time might give me a chance to do something—anything. I didn't know what. But if I could stall for time...

"You're going to write a confession saying that you killed Ralph Pentron, and then Betty Waters because she knew about it," Leiver announced, grinning.

"You don't think that this will hold, do you?" I asked.

"Why not? We got this honest police officer here to back up the story!" He grinned at me. "See what I mean?"

"So, I see. But how're you going to get me to write it?"

"Simple. Bert!"

Without having any pre-warning to defend myself, I felt a terrible blow slice across my face and then another jab into my gut.

☛Chapter Twenty-Eight☚

Somehow I managed to keep standing, but the whole world was spinning around me in a wild mad whirl. Red was flashing before my eyes. Finally I focused through the dizziness and then my wind slowly returned.

"See what I mean, Benton?" Leiver asked. "Think you want to push me?"

I looked at him and then at Bert. There wasn't anything that I could do except as they demanded. One way or the other I'd have to write the damned thing; it would be easier to do it now, before they had a chance to hamburger me into a blubbering chunk of pain and agony.

"Okay, where's the—"

There was a knock on the door.

"Who's that?" Leiver demanded, looking at Larson. Then he smiled. "Sorry, that would have to be Davidson."

Davidson? I felt a shock jolt through my whole body. I couldn't believe it. Davidson? What the hell was he doing here? Why?

"Bert, answer the door!" Leiver demanded.

A moment later Davidson stepped into the room. His face was grim. He motioned toward Larson.

"Grab him!" he demanded, glancing toward Leiver and Bert.

Bert moved fast, as if propelled by an atomic reactor. Before Larson could get the gun from his shoulder holster, Bert had gripped his arm in his thick strong hands.

"Take the gun from him!" Davidson ordered.

"What the hell's going on?" Larson demanded.

"Oh, come on, cut the bull. You know as well as I do." Davidson's voice was harsh and biting. His expression

139

was icy cold. It wasn't the man I'd known for years. I couldn't believe what was happening.

There was a long silence in the room while Davidson slowly turned in my direction, For a moment he looked thoughtfully at me; there was almost a sadness in his eyes, then they hardened and his lips began to move silently. After a few seconds he said, "I tried to get you off my back.

"Why didn't you do like I told you, Dan?"

"I don't get it!" I snapped, still not wanting to believe the obvious.

"I did everything I could to warn, you about—" He broke off and continued an instant later. "You're a hard-headed fool, Dan Benton. If you weren't such a hard-headed fool I still might be able to get you out of this alive—but that's impossible. You understand that—don't you?"

For a moment I didn't say anything. I was still trying to add things up—to overcome the shock of Davidson walking in. But suddenly it did make sense. Somehow it made good sense—in a way.

"Mind telling me about it?" I asked.

"What?" Davidson countered, a little confused.

"Oh, come on, Bill. The set up. If you plan on killing me—"

Larson broke in. "Take it easy, Benton. It won't do you any good!"

Davidson turned toward the police lieutenant. "And you, Mr. Secret-super-spy Larson, I think that we can take care of you, too."

"How'd you find out?" was the man's only reply.

"Oh, that wasn't so hard. Once I realized that I'd made a mistake with Pentron, then it was just a matter of putting two and two together. The thing that puzzled me was that Pentron wouldn't go to the police. If he were working for them, as I believed, there wasn't any reason for him not to go to them. The thing was that Leiver had a grudge against him because of Betty Waters. The fact was that Pentron was just a dopey. Nothing more. In trouble. You see, once I figured out a few facts, it was easy to figure that you had to be the government man. You being on the in with us and working for the government, it put you in a perfect position to get us exactly where they wanted us. The only thing is that it didn't work."

I was puzzled for only a moment. Then everything seemed to slide together. Larson working for the government. The "police contact" that Leiver had talked about. The only thing was that Larson was walking a tightrope. One false move.

"How'd you get on to me?" Larson asked, still surprised.

"I told you. If Pentron wasn't the man, then somebody else had to be. One: you knew that Benton here had been framed. Yet you went after him like you really meant it. Two: you knew that Betty Waters—"

"No I didn't...I didn't know that Benton had been framed!" Larson announced, "At first I thought he might have been one of your men. It was simple enough to figure that you'd sent him out to kill Pentron...the only thing was that you didn't—"

Suddenly I burst into the conversation. Still shocked. "So that's it. You really thought that I was working for Davidson, especially when he pulled me out. So you figured that I was working for—"

"That dirty son-of-a-bitch!" Leiver cried in anger at Larson. "You played both ends against the middle."

"Of course," Davidson pointed out in his silky calm voice. "He played it smart. As a policeman, behind the scene, he could do anything he wanted, and we wouldn't really know anything about it. If we found out that he was putting the squeeze play on one of our boys, he could simply say that it was all an act—a show. Simple. But it's all over now!"

"What do we do with them, boss?" Leiver asked.

"Kill them. And the woman, too."

"No—leave her alone!" Larson begged. "Please leave her—"

"You know we can't do that!" Davidson said in a smooth voice. "She knows too much!"

"Why kill me?" I asked, trying to play for time. "Maybe I'd be interested in going into your deal!"

Davidson smiled. "No—you forget that I've known

141

you for much too long a time. You're too clean. And we're playing for big stakes. You might call us flesh peddlers. Narcotics. A real big deal. And you just aren't the type of person who would do anything like that. You know it and you know that I know it. Stop stalling for time!" He paused and then said: "Take care of them!"

☛Chapter Twenty-Nine☚

Leiver and Bert stepped forward, dragging Larson and the woman with them.

Just then there was the sound of a siren.

"What's that?" Leiver demanded, looking at Davidson.

Bert turned in the direction of the siren. All attention was momentarily away from me. If there was ever to be any chance at all, this was it. If I had to die, then I might as well do it in a fight. At least that way I had a chance. Any other way I didn't have any possible chance.

I swung my arm around at Bert; it was a brutal chopping action, smashing into the side of his neck. He went down with that one punch. Then I leaped for Leiver, the one man that I figured I had to watch out for. Leiver was too smooth and slick and fast on the action. Davidson wasn't something to worry about—yet!

I caught Leiver on the point of the jaw. But he didn't go down. At the same time I saw out of the corner of my eye a gun lying on the television table; I recognized it as my own, and decided to make a play for it. Swinging again at Leiver, this time a slicing blow at his neck, judo style, I leaped toward the table. Whipped up the gun and aimed at Leiver—while at the same time looking for Lieutenant Larson. I spotted Larson on the floor, out cold—somebody had given him the one-two.

The time it took me to see all that gave Bert time to climb to his feet, a gun in hand. He fired before I could turn in his direction.

Pain burned into my left arm. Then I felt another ugly blow as another bullet sliced the side of my head. For a moment I thought I was going to pass out of the picture. Somehow I managed to squeeze the trigger of the gun in my hand. The bullet made contact with Bert's stomach. He exploded backwards. Then I turned around and fired at Davidson, but the shot went wild.

He returned the fire—missing.

Leiver was climbing to his feet at this time, and a shot exploded from the gun in his hand. I turned again and fired in his direction. I saw him jerk backwards and smash into a chair, a surprised hurt expression twisting his face in agony. Blood was oozing from his chest where my bullet had entered. Then a red trickle dripped from his dying lips.

I didn't wait to see the rest of his death agonies. I quickly turned toward Davidson, just as he fired at the now rising Lieutenant Larson. Out of the corner of my eye I could see the policeman fall backwards. I didn't have time to see if he had been killed or just wounded.

The front door suddenly smashed inward.

Davidson made his move then; so fast and unexpectedly that I didn't have time to do anything at first. I fired, but wildly.

His gun was pointed toward me. My second shot exploded in the wall next to him. He returned the fire, but missed.

I heard Mrs. Larson cry: "Oh, God!" in a tormented voice.

Just then several policemen burst into the room, and behind them I saw Sherry.

Suddenly Davidson made a quick move toward Mrs. Larson, grabbing her and pulling the woman in front of him.

"Don't move—any of you!" he ordered, pointing the gun at her head. "One move and she gets it—first!"

He started moving toward the back entrance, pulling Mrs. Larson after him. "Don't do anything, or she gets it!" he cried again.

Sherry moved into the room slowly and stepped to my side. "Are you...oh, God, you're hurt!"

I brushed her aside. Of all times for her to be worrying about a small flesh wound. But that was a woman for you.

144

Nobody did anything as Davidson stepped out of the room. Then I pushed forward.

"Don't!" I heard somebody shout out after me, but I ignored it. I wanted Davidson—and good! I'd been pushed around by a man who had posed as a friend—and that hurt. And there was another motive; he was possibly the only one who could clear me of the murder raps—if Larson was dead. I didn't have time to check, and wasn't about to take it.

I had to get them back. One of them, at least.

I saw a dark shadowy form move across the backyard as I stepped out onto the porch.

A gun spat flame and a bullet fanned the air near my head. I didn't dare fire back. The only chance I had was to be a moving target and let him empty his gun at me, hoping he continued to miss.

Running forward in the zigzagging fashion I'd learned in the Army years before, I rushed forward toward Davidson and Mrs. Larson.

Another shot exploded into the night. It went wild. A third and fourth followed.

"It's not going to do you any good!" I shouted. "You can't get out!"

He didn't answer. Instead he moved away. I suddenly saw his destination—a back gate.

I was only a few yards away from him when he fired again. The bullet smashed through my coat, just skinning my flesh.

I fell forward, moaning. But at the same time I brought my gun up in the direction of Davidson. I kept rolling to one side. I kept my eyes on him and Mrs. Larson. The woman was in an angle away from my line of fire and he didn't have a chance to pull her between me and himself. I fired once. The bullet ripped into his shoulder, twisting him around.

Then I leaped to my feet and rushed at Davidson. My fist shot across his face. Then I aimed a rabbit punch into the side of his neck.

He doubled over, but didn't go down for the count. Instead, he swung with all his strength, slashing my face. I jerked backwards from the stinging blow, and he followed it with one brutal kick into the face.

I was stunned for a moment. Not able to get my bearings. I shook my head and forced myself to a standing position.

Looking around I saw Davidson running down the back alley. My gun was still clutched in my hand.

"Stay where you are, Bill!" I shouted, aiming the weapon in his direction. The idea of killing a man I'd known for so many years—in cold blood—didn't appeal to me; but it wouldn't stop me, either.

He didn't stop.

I fired.

He stumbled and fell. I rushed toward him. When I got to his side, he was struggling to stand.

"Keep it nice and easy!" I demanded.

He looked up at me with frightened eyes; the whites were large and bright in the moonlight. Then he smiled and stood.

"You don't have any more bullets in that gun," he announced, stepping closer to me and swinging a brutal blow at my face. I ducked and returned the attack. My fist jolted the point of his nose, spurting blood over his mangled face.

He moaned and fell backwards. I followed him, ramming my gun-point into the pit of his stomach.

He groaned and slumped to the ground.

At the same time the police came running up. They surrounded me.

"You're under arrest!" one of them announced.

I looked at him in amazement, not able to believe my ears. "What the hell?"

"For the murder of Pentron and Miss Waters," the stiff-faced officer announced grimly

It was too funny for words. I just laughed. Laughed until a voice that I recognized, with a start, as Lieutenant Larson, said: "Forget it, Jed."

I sobered and looked at the man standing in front of me. It was Lieutenant Larson. I couldn't think of anything to say. It seemed as if both of us had been wrong about each other, and there didn't seem anything to say, at first. Then finally I sighed, and extended my hand. "Sorry!"

146

He grinned and took my hand: "Guess we both were wrong. Nice work!"

Then he turned his attention to the policemen giving them orders

Sherry stepped up then.

"Are you all right?" she asked.

I just nodded, taking her arm and pulling her closer. "For the shape I'm in, I feel great!"

We stood there for a long time, not saying anything. Then Lieutenant Larson stepped up.

"There'll be a doctor around pretty soon. We both need some work done on our bodies!" he said, half grinning. "I'm sorry about being on your back so much. But I really thought you were working for Davidson. Then when you showed up tonight at my place—and said what you did—I knew the truth, but couldn't say anything. This was pretty important business. The government men were on to Davidson's activities, but couldn't really pin anything on the man. They asked me to start playing ball with him. Make a few contacts—the whole bit—over a year ago. And then suddenly you stepped in at the climax." He sighed then. "But everything came out in the wash."

SOFTLY AS I KILL YOU, BY CHARLES NUETZEL

❧ Epilog ❧

Several hours later, after the doctor had looked over the couple of scratches that I had gotten in the blow-up, I was sitting next to Sherry in my car. She was behind the driver's seat, waiting for me to give her the word on where to go.

"How about a drink?" I suggested.

She looked strangely at my eyes. "Don't you have something to say to me?"

"What?" I asked, stupidly.

"Well, the cops didn't come on their own!"

I jerked in surprise.

"Of course! How did they happen along?" Everything had happened so fast that I hadn't even given them a thought.

"Well, big boy Benton, I called Davidson and when he wasn't in I called the police. I figured that you'd be heading for Larson's and I was afraid of what might happen."

I thought for a moment and then said: "Thanks!"

She laughed. "Well, let's get going for that drink now!"

She started the engine and glided the car down the darkened street.

That was Sherry: direct and simple and intelligent. That's why I like her for a secretary. And naturally because of all the other extras that she gives her boss. Like "overtime."

And we had a lot of overtime to put in, now. What I needed most of all was a good cocktail and a good girl in a good old-fashioned apartment. I had the girl at my side, right then.

Thirty minutes later I had all the rest.

☛About the Author☚

Charles Nuetzel was born in San Francisco in 1934, and writes:

"As long as I can remember I wanted to be a writer. It was a dream I never thought would materialize. But with the help of Forrest J Ackerman, who became my agent, I managed to finally make it into print.

"I was lucky enough not only in selling my work to publishers but also ending up packaging books for some of them, and finally becoming a 'publisher' much like those who had bought my first novels. From there it as a simple leap to editing not only a sci-fi anthology, but a line of sci-fi books for Powell Sci-Fi back in the 1960s. Throughout these active professional years I had the chance to design some covers and do graphic cover layouts for pocket books & magazines."

Much of his work in covers and graphics are a result of having had a father who was a professional commercial artist, and who did a number of covers for sci-fi magazines in the 1950s and later for pocket books—even for some of Mr. Nuetzel's books.

In retirement he has become involved in swing dancing, a long time lover of Big Band jazz. But more interestingly world travels have taken him (and his wife Brigitte) across the world, to Hawaii, Caribbean, Mexico, Kenya, Egypt, Peru, having a life-long interest in ancient civilizations. His website is full of thousands of pictures taken during these trips.